## The Haunting of
## Jessica Raven

# The Haunting of Jessica Raven

## ANN HALAM

A Dolphin
Paperback

Published in paperback in 1994
by Orion Children's Books
a division of The Orion Publishing Group Ltd
Orion House
5 Upper St Martin's Lane
London WC2H 9EA

Reprinted in 1995, 1996, 1997

First published in Great Britain in 1994
by Orion Children's Books

A catalogue record for this book is available
from the British Library.

Typeset by Deltatype Ltd, Ellesmere Port, Cheshire
Printed in Great Britain by Clays Ltd, St Ives plc

ISBN 1 85881 069 8

# One

$F$ ROM THE WAY THE SILVER SLUG DROVE ON TO THEIR pitch, Jess could tell who was driving (Dad); and that something had 'gone bad', as her little brother Paddy would say. Mum and Dad had taken Adam out for a drive. She'd been jealous, but she supposed it was fair for Adam to get all of Mum and Dad's attention sometimes.

Jessica had been left alone with Paddy all afternoon. It had been a tiring few hours. She'd taken him swimming, and played with him in the campsite playground. She'd tried hard to interest him in some other English-speaking kids who were there, but Paddy had refused to go off and play with his own kind. He insisted on having his sister's company. They'd spent most of the time hanging about on their *emplacement*, as the French call a camping pitch, while kids teemed around, yelling and crashing through the Ravens' territory on their candy-coloured miniature mountain bikes . . . She watched as Dad fidgeted unhappily at the parking of the Slug, feeling her relief at the return of the others drain away. She was sure that the drive had not been a success. At last a silver door opened. Mum appeared, dropped down on to the grass like an exhausted bird, made for Jessica's blue tent in blind, determined strides, and disappeared inside. Paddy squawked 'Mum!' and jumped up, scattering playing cards. They'd been playing Snap. '*Siddown*.' Jessica ordered, in a double-strength snarl to make it stick. 'Leave her alone, you fool.'

Dad came over, and the first thing he saw of course was the washing-up from lunch lying by the camp-kitchen.

'Oh, Jess! he groaned.

'I haven't had *time*,' she protested. 'Paddy's made me play with him *every moment*.'

'Well, get it done before your mother sees it. She's upset enough –' He stared at the washing-up bowl, going into one of his mid-sentence silences: a habit that drove Jess crazy. 'I've got to help Adam.'

'*I'll* help Adam.'

'No,' said Dad. 'No . . .' (a silence). 'Do the dishes.'

Jessica bullied Paddy into picking up the cards. 'This is my holiday,' whimpered the little boy. 'You're making it horrible.'

Jess usually melted when Paddy whimpered. She was too soft-hearted to stay firm when the tough little-boy voice developed that wobble of approaching tears. But the injustice of this accusation disgusted her. 'What about *my* holiday?' she demanded.

She left him lifting up cards incredibly slowly from the groundsheet, one by one, and piling them into a muddled heap. She looked into the blue tent. The dim air inside smelled of proofed nylon, of anti-midge citronella and warm damp grass: the smell of every summer they'd spent in France. Her mother was lying on Jess's airbed, face buried in the rolled sleeping-bag.

'Mum? Are you all right? Can I get you anything?'

Jess's mother lifted her head. 'I'm fine,' she said, in the cold, sarcastic tone that meant she was nearly crying. 'Just fine. My eldest child, my *first born son*, is dying slowly and I can do nothing to save him. Sometimes I get miserable about this. It's my way of coping. Give me some *peace*. For *a few minutes*. Okay?'

'Okay,' said Jess helplessly.

Jess took the washing-up to their nearest sanitaires, trudging through the grey warmth of the at-least-it's-not-raining August afternoon. The weather had been awful all this holiday, which had not helped. The blocks were big and painted bright yellow, with a pink trim. They were scattered over the campsite like huge pastel toys, and every one was identical. They were always busy. She was glad to find an outside washing-up sink free. She filled the vast metal bowl, the clatter of French house-wife-and-children talk babbling around her. Candy-coloured bikes streamed by. Throngs of people in candy-coloured clothes filled the paved paths, that wound between rows of caravans and four-bedroomed tents. On either side of her, stacks of gleaming pans and plates piled up. Someone was scrubbing complicated barbecue equipment, with a cleanser that stank of ammonia.

Jess thought of camping *au sauvage* in the woods. Of living on bread and fruit and pâté, and washing up in a stream. Of birdsong and silence. The Ravens used to despise big, crowded sites like this. Mum used to call them five-star refugee camps. They would begin to plan their vagabond summer in January: first deciding on a route and then rejecting out of hand anything that looked like a holiday-camp site on their way. They would pore over the dog-eared Michelin camping guide in their gloomy London kitchen, picking out the places with one mountain – which meant very basic facilities. If possible they avoided anywhere that provided electricity, because *electricity means caravans, and caravans mean crowds*. They fell with delight on the words *aire naturelle*, which meant a site that was isolated and beautiful, and had few modern conveniences. Often when you reached these spots you found the natural beauty had been exaggerated, but the Ravens didn't care. They'd rather stay somewhere basic in the ordinary French countryside, than languish in scenic luxury with a bar, *supermarché*, restaurant, washing machines, ponyrides, tennis courts, grass skiing and baby-listening. No thank you! They didn't want an open-air tourist hotel. They wanted to be wild and free.

But Adam couldn't live like that anymore, not easily. This year the Silver Slug had become part of their lives – a motor caravan adapted for disabled use, and paid for by a charity. Adam had good days and bad days. Sometimes you could hardly tell there was anything wrong. But even on his best days he couldn't manage in his own tent. On his bad days, the motorized wheelchair (also paid for by charity) had to be brought out, and then there was no way to pretend that life was still normal.

Adam had Sales' Myasthenia, a wasting disease that first crippled and then killed its victims. It was rare, it affected boys not girls. It could be inherited, but it could happen at random. It seemed to be a *random mutation* that had hit the Ravens, like a mindless terrorist striking out at no one in particular. Jessica's parents had had no warning. They'd never heard of Sales' Myasthenia until, when Jessica was six and Paddy was a baby, twelve-year-old Adam suddenly needed glasses. Then he had started feeling weak in games, fumbling and dropping things and stumbling for no reason, and a struggle began to find out exactly what was wrong. At last, after many tests, the cruel verdict had come.

Then everyone had been terrified for Paddy. But it turned out, after more tests, that he was safe. He wasn't going to get sick. And Jessica . . . well, for a long time, Jessica had been forgotten. She still felt that way sometimes, though she knew her parents did their best. She was healthy, normal: and lost. She'd grown up fast, in some ways. In some ways, she felt that her life had stopped.

She pushed a limp pale strand of hair back from her face. It was damp from the weary time she'd spent in the campsite *piscine*, with Paddy and a splashing, yelling horde of five-star refugees. She was afraid it was turning green again. Swimming-pool water always made Jess's hair turn green: it was the chlorine.

*My eldest child, my first born son.*

It hurt when Mum said things like that, as if only Adam mattered. Jess tried not to mind. Mum didn't mean it to hurt. One of the first things you learn, thought Jess, when something terrible comes to roost in your life, is not to mind the awful things people say when they are miserable . . . She knew she'd come out with some crackers herself, from time to time.

*I wish he was dead now. I can't stand another ten years of this. Why can't he go and live in a home?*

Something poked her in the back.

'Hi, green-eyes,' said Adam. 'Came to see if I can help.'

He was on his feet, leaning on the antique walking-stick he'd bought for himself a year ago. It wasn't really much use, because if he was feeling weak his hands were weak too. He had some grim-looking crutches that were more effective. But he liked his stick. He poked its fierce ferrule into the turf, and held out his hands.

'Toss me a tea-towel, I'll dry.'

Adam's eyes were green like Jess's, as far as you could

see them through the pebble lenses. His hair was dark: as crisp and thick and curly as Jessica's was limp and straight. Jessica remembered the first time he'd had to go into hospital. She'd been so afraid that he'd come back a weird-looking bald-stranger. He didn't, but she knew now that it wouldn't matter. Whatever happened he would still be Adam, her best friend. He was the only person Jess completely trusted in the entire world.

She handed him the cloth and passed plates, one by one and carefully: not because they would break – they were indestructible – but because Adam hated dropping things. He looked up and down the row of shiny sinks, and mugged a goofy sad face. Adam too often knew exactly what Jess was thinking.

'Not much like *Swallows and Amazons*, is it?'

Jess shrugged, ashamed of herself. 'Oh, it's okay. I could get used to having hot water to wash up in. And a sink you don't have to plug with grass. Did you have a good afternoon?'

She had wanted to change the subject, but at once she wished she hadn't asked. Obviously they *hadn't* had a good time, or Mum wouldn't be lying in Jess's tent, in a grief-stricken heap.

'Not too bad,' said Adam, carefully examining the back of a plate. 'We didn't do much, we drove around for miles looking at the pretty countryside. Sorry, Jess. This is a reject. A large lump of spag bog sauce has escaped your expert attention.'

'Paddy's been a real pain,' complained Jess, taking the plate (thinking: all right, don't tell me what went wrong for Mum). 'I was hoping I'd get a chance to sunbathe and have a quiet read, while you were doing the boring sightseeing. But he wouldn't leave me alone. Why does he want to be with me all the time? I'm *thirteen*, I'm a *girl*! He should hate the sight of me!'

Adam looked her up and down, and laughed. 'Face it, green-eyes. The kid's got taste. You're kind and you're funny and he trusts you. You'll have to change your ways if you want to scare him off. Besides, look at the competition! Nothing but foreign loons in dire pink lycra bulges, far as the eye can see.'

The woman at the next sink was clad in pink lycra cycle shorts and bikini top. So was her little daughter, who was staring at Adam's walking stick with childish, inoffensive interest. They were both generously built.

*'Adam!'* hissed Jess, appalled.

'What's matter?'

*'She might understand English!'*

'So what? They aren't going to attack a poor cripple. Besides, I have my trusty sword-stick, I fear nothing.'

She giggled. 'It's not a sword-stick!'

Adam rolled his eyes. 'Ah, but they don't know that!'

When they'd finished Jess carried the stacked bowl back to the pitch, walking slowly at Adam's pace: tremendously comforted by his teasing, his wickedness, his *being there*. Dad had made hot lemon tea. Dad said hot tea was the most refreshing drink you could have in the heat: lemon tea was a habit they'd got into when they were roughing it and had no caravan fridge to keep the milk fresh. The sky had cleared and the sun was suddenly rich and roasting. Mum was herself again. She spread jam on biscuits, cheerfully talking to Dad about what there was to cook this evening. That was the best thing about Mum, her storms never lasted. She plunged into dreadful depths, but she didn't brood. She came up again brave and smiling. You could rely on that.

Paddy had started to built a town out of pebbles on the groundsheet, using playing cards to pave the road between his lumpy stone houses. Jessica lay alongside the city limits: a dozing giant, munching jam biscuit and sipping hot sweet tangy tea. Paddy drove a car over her bare side, making the droning noise of its engine. He sounded like a bumblebee. 'Jess,' said Mum, 'Have you put on plenty of sunscreen? The sun's strong when it comes out for a moment. Did you remember your strap marks?'

'Yes Mama. I did, Mama.'

Mum didn't believe it. She fetched the Factor 15. The giant put down her tea and Mum smoothed cream into her shoulders: smoothing away the hurt of that cry of *My eldest child, my first born son.* I love you, said Mum's hands. I love you as much as I love Adam or Paddy, and I always will.

Jess squinted up through her lashes at the woods that surrounded the campsite, and at the château: the big fat towers that looked down from over the tree-tops. 'Are we going up there, to the *donjon?*' she asked sleepily, feeling good and normal and happy again. 'Are we going to see the castle?'

'Why not?' said Dad. 'It'll cost an arm and a leg, but why not? Since we're here. We'll go tomorrow.'


The castle was called the Château des Rochers-Jumeaux. It was really two castles, built on the tops of two crags that rose above the modern town of Rochers. They were joined by a bridge that spanned the gorge of a little rushing river. The Tour de Garde, which was the castle on the eastern rock, had no water. If people were besieged there and the bridge was broken, there was a secret passage through the crag, so the defenders could sneak down and get water from the river. It had been used as an administration centre by the Nazis, and destroyed by fire at the end of the Second World War. It was ruined now. The western keep, the Tour des Eaux, which used to be the ruined part, had been completely restored.

In the Terror, during the French Revolution, the castle had been sacked by the local peasantry, and many treasures had been lost . . .

Jess read these interesting facts on an information board (printed in three languages), in the car-park on top of the western crag, while Dad and Mum and Adam were buying tickets. The negotiations were still going on when she'd read all she wanted. She went to haul Paddy away from the souvenir stalls, where he was going into his usual feeding-frenzy over the toys.

'You don't want a car,' she told him sternly. 'They're the same as toy cars at home. Why don't you buy a proper souvenir?'

'I'll get an ice lolly. Theirs are different.'

'Don't waste your money. There'll be a free one, I mean a parents-money one, on a gig like this.'

She had half an eye on what was happening at the castle gates. Dad was holding up the queue while he made sure that there'd be plenty of things Adam could do. Jessica hated this part of getting in anywhere. Adam was very tired today, and in the wheelchair. But why did Dad have to keep asking questions? Its was true, 'disabled access' often turned out to be a hollow pretence. But Jess would prefer, and she was sure Adam would prefer it too, for them to find that out in private, for themselves . . .

'Come on, they're going in.'

The guide had come out of her ticket booth to open a wider door in the huge towering gates. She ushered the Ravens in, and gave them a plan on which she'd marked the wheelchair route. She explained carefully how to reach the place where you could take the *ascenseur* to the state apartments, where the tour began.

Mum and Dad spoke cheerfully bad French. Adam was better. Jessica understood nearly everything anyone said, but she choked up when she tried to speak it aloud. She translated this last part for Paddy. He was astonished.

'A lift! Did they have lifts in middle-evil days?'

'You say that word "mediaeval". It'll be a modern lift. Why not? People still use these châteaux, same as people still live in stately homes in England.'

Paddy's face fell a mile. 'I'll wait in the car-park.'

'What's the *matter*?'

'You said there was a dungeon. I wanted to see the torture things. There can't be olden torture things if there's a lift.'

'I said there was a *donjon*, idiot. The big fat towers are the *donjons*. Dungeons are called something else.' But he looked so wounded by the prospect of a castle without horrors, that she relented. 'I'm sure there's a torture chamber. We'll find it.'

They passed through the thickness of the wall, into a vast expanse of cobbled yard. The crowd of visitors around them spread out and seemed to vanish. Jessica looked up and around, staggered by the size of everything. There must have been a whole army of people living in here, when the citadel was in working order.

The yard was set up for the *son et lumière*, the historical pageant that would be put on here tonight. The town and all the roadsides round about were plastered with posters for this show. The Ravens wouldn't be going, the tickets were too expensive. Paddy knew this. But he had been excited by the posters, which showed a gory and realistic-looking beheading on stage. So his family hurried him on: past the wooden stage, the scaffolding hung with floodlights, the tiers of seats.

They found the menagerie. It had once been a regular zoo, with lions, tigers and a real rhinoceros. Mum and Dad and Adam went to check out the times of the guided tour, while Jess led Paddy around pens of guinea pigs and rabbits and goats and Vietnamese pigs. She discovered that the French for guinea pig, is *cobaye*. The tortoises (*tortues*) were being fed. The keeper had a sack of soft, floppy yellow things which he was tossing over the wall while children around him gasped gleefully. Jess wondered, what kind of lettuce is yellow? When they were close she saw that the tortoises were being fed on *dead baby chicks*.

Paddy was ecstatic. Jess turned away, disgusted. In spite of the cropped hedges and bright flowerbeds, she thought there was still a faint stink of large beasts imprisoned: a hopeless, dank sort of smell. The great walls loomed over everything. The sky, which was blue today but still felt heavy and close, seemed fixed overhead like the lid of a box. Maybe it was because Jess didn't like zoos, but she began to feel that she didn't like the château. It must have been horrible to live here; like being in prison.

When they joined the others Mum and Dad were arguing about the picnic sandwiches, in the way parents argue when they're really fighting about something that can't be mentioned in front of the children. Jessica didn't want to go on the guided tour. She thought it was madness to take Paddy along to stare at fancy French furniture and pictures, in the 'state apartments'. But the tour was paid for – it was in with the price of the tickets – and Dad was in one of his dumb-obstinate moods. So it had to be. The Ravens trailed along to the lift: Paddy excited because he thought he was going to see torture chambers, Mum and Dad still snapping, Adam's chair humming like a wasp while Adam sat wearily silent.

'I *told* you to use the pâté, Chris –'

'I don't know what's wrong with cheese –'

'It was for the *pasta*. Do I have to do everything!'

Without knowing quite what had gone wrong, Jessica

felt the outing to the château turning into one of those sad holiday failures, preserved forever in the family's miserable expressions, in the pictures of this famous château that had to be stuck in the album . . . The lift was in a kind of mediaeval underpass. Beside it there was a broad pit in the floor, covered with a metal grille.

'Dungeons!' whooped Paddy. But they cruelly dragged him away, before he could get his head stuck or pitch himself down the hole.

'It's probably only the well,' Jess consoled him.

The tour began in the state banqueting hall. It was a big room with a long polished table down the middle, set for a meal that would never happen, like something in a doll's house. On the walls there were rows of pictures in gold frames, so many of them that they all looked the same. The guide droned on and on. Her victims stood in a cowed huddle. If anyone fidgeted or coughed, she fixed them with a ferocious glare.

She seemed mostly to be saying that everything they would see in the castle was fake. It was all restored, nothing was real, none of the fancy furniture belonged here, nobody had ever been tortured in the dungeons . . . Jess wanted to whisper to Adam that the bit about nobody being tortured was clearly untrue! But Adam seemed to have gone to sleep: his head was bowed, his eyes half-closed. Paddy was staring at the crystal and gilt tableware as if someone had hypnotized him. He'd probably gone into one of his counting trances, he loved counting things. Jessica was so bored it hurt. She glanced at the leaflet she was holding, and saw ahead of her reams of this agony: the armoury, the kitchens, the *cachots* (that meant real dungeons, Paddy would be pleased); the Museum of the Resistance . . . Yuck, more torture-relics.

*I cannot stand this*, she decided.

Without giving herself time for second thoughts, and *especially* without catching Mum or Dad's eye, she suddenly but quietly broke out of the huddle of visitors, and made for the great double-leaved doors.

Once she was outside, she didn't know what to do. She didn't want to be alone. She wanted to be with Adam. She wanted to sneak off and see if they could cross the bridge over the gorge, which was closed to the public – the most exciting places always are, in castles. They used to do things like that. Adam was lawless, even after he started to get sick: lawless and yet so *sensible*, so competent, that when he got them into trouble the adults could never really put him down. But those times were over now.

She thumbed the leaflet. What else did this place have to offer? She didn't want to buy a souvenir, or see the aquarium, or the musée of local history, or the diorama of the Battle of Crècy. She definitely did not want to see photos of what resistance fighters looked like after a weekend with the Gestapo. In the end she just wandered through the rest of the state apartments: and on, along a wide, uncarpeted passageway beyond the public rooms. At last she came to another double-leaved door. She pushed one side open, and found herself looking into a silent, cool dazzle of colour. The air smelt of stone and beeswax. It was the chapel.

When her eyes got used to the dimness she saw slender columns and fat pillars, rising through shadow. The far-off roof was netted over with delicately branching stone. There were a few small electric lamps in candle sconces along the walls. Patches of fruit-drop colour lay on the floor, under the narrow stained-glass windows. The columns were coloured in lozenges of blue and rose, wound around with painted silver garlands. The fat pillars that alternated with them were painted with people – saints, she supposed – and flowers and animals. Other saints – statues – stood in niches. The vault overhead was blue between the stone branches, scattered with gold and silver stars.

There was one other visitor, an elderly man. He was on his knees in the shadows at the back, either actually praying or having a moment's peace. Jess walked quietly. She read in the English pages of her leaflet that none of this faded riot of colour was really old. It was a copy – done in 1887 – of what the decoration would have looked like in mediaeval times, when the chapel was new.

She felt cheated. Everything in this castle seemed to be restored or copied. Nothing was ancient, nothing was *real*. She reached the altar steps. A red lamp glowed, hanging down over the altar on a silver chain. There was a smell of old incense. She moved off to the left, where the leaflet said there was a fourteenth-century statue of the virgin in the lady-chapel. Something really old, at last! Candles flickered in a wrought-iron stand. Jess sat down on one of the rush-seated chairs.

The statue was one of the kind called a 'Black Virgin', because of the dark wood used for the carving. She was small and fat, wrapped in a thick cone of dark gold-embroidered brocade and wearing a gilded crown that seemed too big for her. She was holding something in her hands, a sort of spiky wreath that glittered with colour. She held it above the head of the child who was sitting on her lap. She was called the Virgin of the Chaplet (*Couronne*) . . . The *couronne* (that must mean the wreath-thing, decided Jess, reading the leaflet . . .) *on display is a nineteenth-century copy in glass and base metal. The original, which was a treasure of enormous value due to the size and quality of the stones, was lost in the Terror.*

Ha! Typical! thought Jess.

But somehow the Black Virgin, with her child's

imitation jewelled crown, tugged at Jess's heart. So many people, if the leaflet was right, had believed in that funny little fat woman's powers, had knelt here and prayed: *please, take the bad thing away. Don't let the disaster happen to me*. The Ravens didn't go to church, they weren't religious. If they'd considered turning to God for comfort, because of what happened to Adam, Jess had never heard her parents mention it. She thought Mum, at any rate, would be too proud. But of course they prayed. Everybody prays.

Jess had prayed herself. She prayed that she would become a famous molecular biologist, and discover a cure for Adam's disease. She had tried to bargain with whatever power had struck her brother down, offering her life (I won't get married, I'll have no children, I'll dedicate myself to my research . . .) in return for his. She knew it wouldn't work, but the reckless offer made her feel better, sometimes.

She realized suddenly that this day, this spoiled outing, was spoiled because Mum and Dad and Adam had for once given up the hard work they did; the invisible work of being cheerful and pretending everything was normal. They had lost heart. *I haven't been helping*, she thought. But I'll be better. All I needed was a chance to sit down, a chance to breathe.

She was still gazing at the madonna, but in fact she'd forgotten about the statue. Her mind was empty, and quiet as the chapel. The jewelled *couronne* began to glow. It lifted from the virgin's hands and hung in the air. Each faceted element, marvellously distinct, was made so as to fit into the next with exquisite accuracy. Jess had no idea that any jeweller could do that sort of carving: linking emeralds, rubies, diamonds . . . *It's beautiful!* she cried. *It's beautiful* . . .

She started. The glowing circlet had gone. The Black

Virgin held out her chain of coloured glass and rather tarnished metal, as before. Jess felt as if she'd woken with a jolt from a vivid dream. She looked around quickly. She was afraid she'd yelled aloud, but she couldn't have done: the elderly visitor in the back hadn't stirred. As she looked, he got up unhurriedly, crossed himself and left.

'Stupid,' muttered Jess. 'I'm going nuts. Maybe it's the incense. I'd better get out of here.'

In the courtyard of the Musée de la Résistance, she almost bumped into Adam, who was whizzing across the cobbles at a dangerous rate. He fended her off the chair. 'Hey,' he said. 'Watch out. You'll scratch my paint-work.' He looked at her curiously. 'What's up? Have you seen a ghost?'

'I – I dunno, I might've done.'

'Lucky you. Did you get any clues to the lost treasure?'

'Is there one?'

'In a place like this? There's got to be.'

She remembered that the real crown – 'of enormous value' – had been lost in the French Revolution. This was just like Adam, thinking her own thoughts before she thought them herself. A clue to a lost treasure? Somehow the idea was frightening, not exciting. Before she had time to say more Paddy rushed up.

'We saw *dungeons*!' he yelled. 'And there were people in them, being tortured!' His triumph faded a little. 'They weren't real people,' he admitted. 'They were dummies, dressed up.'

'A very clean set of dungeons,' grinned Adam. 'Disneyland.'

Mum and Dad were there. 'You could go up the tower,' offered Dad. 'They're off up the *donjon* tower now, but we left them to it. We've had enough.'

'But we're coming to the party!' shouted Paddy. 'In the night, in the dark, there's a party with fireworks and crisps and coke and a disco and we're invited!'

'It's the end of the *son et lumière* run,' explained Mum. 'The whole town's involved. On the last night there's a free party for everyone, and the people in the pageant come down in costume after the show. It happens to be tonight, so we're in luck.'

'What? We're coming back here, to the castle?' Jess didn't mean to sound so alarmed.

The others looked puzzled. 'No, no,' said Mum. 'There's a reception for the bigwigs up here in the state apartments. But the party's down in the town. Is that all right, Jess?'

'Picnic! Picnic!' chanted Paddy. 'I'm starving!'

'I've had enough too,' said Jess. 'The party sounds great, let's go and eat.'

So they went to have their picnic, on the highest terrace of the menagerie garden. The cloud had passed. Maybe it was the feeling of achievement, from having survived the guided tour, but for whatever reason Mum and Dad were happy again. Jess told herself that her 'vision' in the chapel had been a combination of a daydream and a trick of the light. She still felt oddly as if she'd had a lucky escape. She was very relieved, though she couldn't have explained exactly why, to think that she'd never be inside these looming walls again.

# Two

*J* ESS COLOURED HER EYEBROWS CAREFULLY IN SMOKY
brown. She used the same soft pencil on her eyelids,
and applied a bit of brown mascara. Mum wouldn't let
her put anything on her actual face ever, except sun-
block. *Save it for when you're forty*, she said, *and you need
it. Cover up your skin, and you'll ruin it fast*. Jess didn't use
lipstick. She thought her mouth must be a strange
colour, she couldn't find a shade that looked better than
none. She loosened her hair, which she'd plaited tight
that morning when it was wet after her shower. It burst
out in a crimped cloud. She ran her fingers through it and
studied the effect: green eyes, well-marked freckles on
the broad, low bridge of her nose.

She sighed resignedly. Being a natural blonde isn't so
wonderful. It means you have white eyebrows, pig's
eyelashes and – most likely – limp hair that gets greasy in
half an hour no matter what you do to it. At least she
wasn't sunburned. Jess's hair was nearly white but it was
Scandinavian fairness, not English: Mum's Mum was
from Finland. Jess didn't burn. The block Mum insisted

on for everyone, was to stop them getting skin cancer from the hole in the ozone-layer.

People were going to be dressed up at the party. Jess was wearing a long white muslin shirt with ruffles, and her black, layered cobweb skirt. She stared at herself and wondered why she was taking all this trouble. She didn't expect to meet anyone. Boys! How could she possibly manage to strike up any chat with a strange French boy?

She'd probably be stuck with Paddy anyway.

Rochers, with its *son et lumière* and its guided-tour castle, wasn't the kind of French town they usually stayed in. It was the sort of place where every street was a pedestrian precinct lined with restaurant tables and antique shops: where even the vegetable stalls on the supposed 'authentic street market' were as expensive as buying your food in Harrods; where everyone local looked at you just long enough to decide how much money you had. Jess secretly yearned after places like Rochers, but Mum would say 'too beautified for us'. She was right. When it came to it, Jess didn't like being ripped off any more than her parents did. You walked the pretty streets of a place like this, you looked at things. Then you ate your sandwiches by the famous ancient church, and drove on to somewhere more human . . .

So why were they here? Jess frowned at herself in the mirror and accepted that she would never know. Just as she would never know what had happened, yesterday, when Mum came back from that drive in tears. She had developed an instinct about not asking questions. Tonight there was the party, which ought to be some kind of fun: and tomorrow they would be on their way.

Back at the *emplacement* Paddy was wearing a black teeshirt that was Jess's and reached his knees: a sash that was a scarf of hers and a black hairband swiped over one eye for a pirate patch. He had his treasured plastic cutlass stuck in his sash, three feathers stuck in the hairband, and he was having fierce red stripes drawn across his nose, with face-paint from the keep-Paddy-happy box. Adam had another of Jess's scarves, a purple and white geometric one, tied round his head in a rakish bandana.

'You look ridiculous,' said Jess. 'Both of you. What are you, Paddy, a pirate or an Apache brave?'

'I'm *both*. I'm a pirate with warpaint.'

Jess laughed. 'Give him a moustache. And don't forget to black out his teeth.'

'Can't. There's nothing to black.' Adam poked the tip of a black face-crayon into the space left by Paddy's departed front milk teeth. 'Can't black a gap.'

'Black out my gap!' yelled Paddy, fell on the ground and started to yelp with laughter. He was crazy about parties.

On this same night of late summer, two hundred years ago, a horde of starving peasants had stormed the gates of the Tour des Eaux and run wild through the citadel of the hated Baron. A reenactment of that event was the grande finale of the yearly *son et lumière*. According to the tour guide in the castle, the Baron had been away. He and his family had left the country before the Revolution reached its height. There'd been no one in the castle but a few servants who mostly escaped with their lives . . . And the 'starving peasants' were probably simply roving robbers, who cared nothing for political injustice. The enactment in the yearly show was an artistic impression, not fact.

But what do tour guides know? Tonight the town of Rochers certainly *felt* like a place that was celebrating something important. The Ravens parked the Silver Slug and joined the crowds that were pouring on to an open space under the western crag. Up above, the show had begun. Speakers hanging from garlanded poles around the ground gave out amplified voices, warlike music and the clash of weapons: there was a battle going on in the tourney yard.

'Strange lights play about the tower of the Citadel,' said Adam. 'What devilry are our masters preparing?' He grinned at Jess. 'It's ironic, isn't it. Here's you and me grovelling down here, while the aristos feast above: just like the old days. The Revolution doesn't seem to have changed things much.' He waved his fist at the *donjon* that loomed over them. 'À bas de la tyrannie!'

'At least we're grovelling for free,' Jess pointed out.

Adam, ruthless in his wheelchair, shoved through the crowd to investigate the buffet tables, where supper was being served at thirty-five francs a head: *charcuterie, salade russe, tarte aux poivres*. He returned and announced that he'd pay not to have to eat it: 'Two slices of dead dog, and a saucer full of sick . . .'

Dad told him not to be xenophobic, which means afraid of foreigners. Adam said he thought it made sense to be afraid of people who ate dead dog and vomit for fun. 'What about English jelly and custard,' countered Jess. 'Skinned slug with slime sauce. What about *trifle*. What about *pressed tongue?* Bleggh!'

'Bleggh!' shrieked Paddy delightedly.

Dad spluttered, while his children mock-retched and giggled.

'Anyway, we've eaten,' said Mum, to calm things down.

Mum and Dad went to buy a bottle of wine from the one of the bar-stalls, and find somewhere to sit. There were chairs set out by the *plan d'eau* – the little lake in the middle of the ground – for the firework display. Jess, who loved fireworks, wanted to go with them to make sure they secured a good view. But suddenly the disco music began and there was no stopping Paddy. He raced for the open-air dancefloor and his brother and sister had to follow, Adam's chair jolting over the turf. They watched their lunatic little brother flinging himself about, rolling on the boards, kicking his legs in the air. Paddy believed he was the coolest mover on earth. He was hysterically funny. It was a shame when the floor started to fill up. The French partygoers – young and old, most of them in fancy dress – were good-humoured about it, but Paddy kept crashing into people. Jess had to plunge in and haul him out.

'I'll take him off,' offered Adam. 'You can stay.'

But she didn't feel like dancing by herself. And there'd be no fun in standing on the edge alone, hoping some stranger she couldn't talk to would ask her to join him.

There were big drums full of ice standing about, stuffed with cans of beer and soft drinks. A beautiful French woman dressed as a black cat, stopped and told them – in English – that the drinks were free, only wine and food had to be paid for. Jess pulled out a can of cola for Paddy, a can of Heineken for Adam. She hesitated. 'Oh, go on,' said her brother. 'It won't do you any harm. Just don't guzzle too many. Or if you do, stick by me. I'd rather have you being sick in my lap than under a bush with some drunken yokel –'

Jess grinned, and pulled out a beer. 'I'll have *one*.'

Pirates and cowboys and Balinese dancers swirled around them, eyes flashing with party make-up, laughing and chattering. The disco music – much improved by the party atmosphere – made it seem as if everyone was dancing.

'Why don't people do things like this at home?' demanded Jess.

'If "people" did, we wouldn't go,' said Adam. 'The

English are too lazy. We'd stay home in front of our tellies.'

It was deepest dusk when they went to find their parents. The day had been hot, for once. The evening was warm, there was a feeling of thunder in the air. Mum and Dad had collared a table and chairs right by the rope that kept people off the lake shore. 'Ne passez pas devant la corde!' said Dad. The beams of flashlights bobbed about, on the floating platform where the fireworks were being prepared. Suddenly, without warning, a tree of silver and green shot up into the air: and down, into the equal darkness of the water. The green and silver fire, re-doubled, blazed in a million sparkling ripples. The crowd on the shore gasped. A flight of rockets went up: gold and red, mirrored magically in the water. Paddy hooted and waved his cutlass.

'I *love it*!' cried Jess. 'Fireworks are my *best* thing!'

She poured the last dribble of her beer down her throat. She didn't think it was affecting her. She was happy anyway. If something terrible comes into your life, there are still perfect moments: and this was one. She leaned contentedly against Adam's chair, for once accepting what the chair meant without bitterness.

She was keeping half an eye on Paddy, who was bound to *passe devant la corde* and fall in the lake if he got the chance. But she forgot him, while three more excellent flights of rockets soared into the night. The next moment, she looked and he was gone.

She caught up with him in the dark beyond the disco.

'Paddy! Come back! You can't go off by yourself!'

He turned, firework light making odd patterns on his war-stripes. 'You can play too,' he said. 'We're sneaking into the pirates' castle.'

'Who's we?'

'Me and my crew. You can join us. Come on.' He'd found a path, that led into the woods round the foot of the crag. He stomped on, a stubborn little figure in a world of his own.

'Pirates don't *have* castles. . . !' protested Jess. 'Come back: we'll miss the fireworks –'

'These ones do. Fireworks aren't an adventure. Let's go. I'm Peter Pan. You can be Wendy.'

That did it. This is what I get, thought Jess grimly, for treating a six-year-old boy like a friend. *He wouldn't learn*, that Jess would not tolerate being stuck with the wimpy girl-parts. She crossed the space between them in two strides, turned him round and grabbed him by the front of his – of *her* – teeshirt.

'Listen, sunshine. I've told you this before. *I am not Wendy*. Wendy's a mass hallucination. She does not exist. *I'm Tinkerbell*. Got that? Mean, nasty Tinkerbell, the fairy with *attitude*. Now *you* come on. Back to the show, before they get worried.'

'M-m-m-ass halloosy-woosy?' Paddy's eyes were bright and defiant, inches from her face. Jess began to shake him – gently: and someone giggled.

They were not alone.

Jess knew from the first moment that the children were trouble. They had emerged silently out of the night. They gathered in a ragged half-circle around Jess and Paddy, staring. Though it was dark out here away from the lights, she could see that they were in fancy dress. They were wearing home-made, olden-days costumes, no particular period: 'breeches' that were their dads' old trousers cut down, 'long dresses' hanging round their ankles, that would have been knee-length on adult women. They had bare feet or wooden clogs. Their eyes and teeth glimmered.

It was a snigger, not a giggle: a cruel sound. It came from a boy of about ten, who stood in front of the others. Some of them looked older but he seemed to be the leader. A lock of dark hair fell over his narrow white face.

'Who are you?' he asked in French.

Jess noticed that they had applied lashings of artistic dirt to go with their costumes – grey smears on noses, heavy grime on hands and knees and clothes. There were plenty of children in fancy dress at the party, but these looked as if they'd actually been in the pageant. That would explain why they seemed so sure of themselves. It didn't explain the nasty tone of the boy's voice.

'Who are *you*?' said Jess, in the same language. 'Why are you staring at us?' She wasn't going to be faced down by a little kid. But the boy frightened her.

The children ignored Jess. They looked at Paddy. *'Tu veux jouer?'* asked the boy with the dark hair. Which meant 'Do you want to play?' But he said it with such a mean, cold smile, you'd think he was inviting a kitten to come and be drowned. He looked like the sort of boy who would enjoy drowning a kitten. Jess had let go of Paddy's shirt. Whether or not he understood the words, he knew he was being invited to join some mischief. He went to the children as if drawn by a magnet. The whole group – there were about twenty of them – started moving up the path.

'Hey,' cried Jess, running up and grabbing her brother. 'What d'you think you're doing? Leave him alone!'

'Don't be afraid,' called a voice from below. 'They're with me.' A boy, or a young man, about Adam's age, appeared.

'I'm in charge,' he said, smiling. 'Everything's fine.'

He was not as tall as Adam. His hair was brown, his eyes were light. His skin was either naturally dark or very tanned. He was grinning, a nice grin with white teeth. Jess looked at him hard and felt that he was not drunk, or dangerous, or a pest.

'I am Jean-Luc,' he said. 'And you?'

Jess suddenly decided that the pageant children couldn't be too bad, if Jean-Luc was their guardian. Mum and Dad probably wouldn't mind if she and Paddy joined in this game. They were always hoping their children would make French friends.

'I'm Jessica Raven. That's my brother Paddy. We're English.'

While Jean-Luc and Jess stood smiling at each other, both – it seemed to Jess – not sure how to start a conversation, the children had set off again up the path into the trees, taking Paddy with them. Jean-Luc exclaimed softly. He didn't need to explain that he was anxious, and that these children were a real handful. Jess felt that she understood everything. They hurried in pursuit.

The children were jostling Paddy and telling each other *ask if he has anything to eat*. She saw that some of them had hunks of some kind of cake or dark bread, which they gnawed at as they climbed. The way they ate reminded Jess of the tortoises in the menagerie. Their jaws moved like machinery, blindly champing, while they kept walking and their eyes flickered everywhere. Someone must have trained them to eat 'like starving peasants', for their part in the *son et lumière*, and they'd learned their lesson well. It was not pleasant to watch. One of them had got hold of Paddy's red Mickey Mouse daypack, which he always carried. She saw a bar of chocolate come out of it and pass swiftly from hand to hand, to the little leader of the gang.

'Hey!' called Jean-Luc, in an angry undertone. 'Marcel! Give that to me!'

The white faced boy said something rude and dodged away, sneering, hands behind his back. 'It's all right,' protested Paddy, appearing at Jess's side. 'I said they could have it. They're hungry, Jess. They're poor children. They can have the bag too if they like.'

'What?' Jess peered at him, unable to make out his expression in the gloom. 'Don't be silly, Paddy. It's a game, they're *acting*, they're in fancy dress. They're not really hungry. Of course they can't have your daypack!'

'I'm sorry,' said Jean-Luc, handing the red pack to Jess. 'They're like little devils sometimes. one must forgive them.'

Branches had closed overhead, they walked in a confusing mesh of shadows and darkness. A rocket hissed into the sky, making Jess jump. The children didn't even glance up. She thought she ought to grab Paddy and get out of this. But Jean-Luc was grinning his shy white grin: and his eyes were admiring. He looked as if he was trying get up the courage to say something like *do you come here often?* – or whatever French boys say. He wouldn't know she was only thirteen.

She realized they'd stopped, grinning foolishly at each other again, and the children had once more disappeared. 'Where's Paddy!' she cried. She ran up the path. Before she'd gone more than a few metres it came to an end. Paddy was there, with the children. They had reached the face of the crag. One of the bigger girls – she had two long braids, she might have been Jess's age, but her face looked old in its make-up of grime – was holding up a swathe of tangled creepers. There was a black hollow underneath. It wasn't a shadow, it was the entrance to a cave or a tunnel.

There was a sharp intake of breath behind her.

'Simone! Be careful, be quick!'

Jean-Luc was there. He was hustling the children into

that darkness: and before she knew it, Jess was being jostled in among them. 'Hey,' she cried, but softly, because she was more confused than annoyed. 'What's going on?'

He didn't answer. He was calling his roll. 'Marcel, Simone, Liliane, Jean-Claude, Jacques, Richard, Lea, Emile, René . . .' The children sniggered and reluctantly answered, some of them with swear-word additions that Jean-Luc ignored. Jess felt a hand slip into hers: it was Paddy.

'Marcel is the boss,' he whispered importantly. 'Richard and René and some of them, and Simone of the girls are all older than him, but he's the chief because there's nothing he wouldn't do. He's killed someone, even. We're sneaking into the dungeons now.'

Jess held the warm damp little hand tightly. Killed someone, indeed, she thought. How ridiculous. Trust Marcel to tell a lie like that, to a six-year-old. What a brat!

'Who told you all that? You can't speak French.'

'I understand them though, sort of.'

'Allons!' hissed Jean-Luc, *Come on!*

'Wait a minute!' protested Jess. 'I don't think –' But Paddy twisted his hand free, so she had to stop protesting and dive after him, into the dark.

'It's all right,' said Jean-Luc close beside her, sounding out of breath. 'Don't be afraid. I'm in charge, all's well.'

But he didn't sound as if all was well. And Jess didn't feel as if he was in charge. Marcel would be bad enough on his own. The others weren't much better. And now they were invisible in the dark, in a passage that seemed to be plunging straight into the side of the hill. Jess was scared. She waited for somene to switch on a torch, but nobody did. She had to go with them, or desert Paddy: there was no choice.

The first passage was a crawl. They came out into a cavern that was shot with faint light from far overhead. It must be coming in through cracks and crevasses in the rock, Jess thought. Her eyes, accustomed to the dark now, made out a wide space, with signs of stonework and old iron brackets on the walls. She spotted Paddy by his blond head, and grabbed him thankfully. To him it was a great game. 'It's the dungeons!' he crowed. 'It's like Adam said. Those ones on the tour were Disneyland! These are real!'

He was probably right. 'Let's go,' she snapped, trying to see the entrance of the tunnel they'd come in by. But the others, Jean-Luc's charges, seemed at home in the dark. They swarmed around the English children, blocking their escape. Jess felt a tug at her waist and yelped: slapped her hands down and caught the tail of the belt of her waist-pouch, as it was whipped away.

'Rachel! You bad girl!' Jean-Luc handed back the pouch. 'A million pardons. They are to be pitied, one must not be angry. They have forgotten how to behave. Say you are sorry, Rachel.'

The little girl, a child scarcely bigger than Paddy, clawed out of Jean-Luc's grip, spitting at him.

'I'm sorry,' he repeated. 'You would not be angry if you knew. One has to accept them as they are.'

No, one has not, thought Jess, furious. Little pigs. One has to lay down the law . . . The children hovered just out of Jean-Luc's reach, giggling. 'Come on,' murmured one of them – was it Simone, the tall girl with the young-old face? She tossed her ratty braids and sneered. 'Share our game. Are you afraid, English?'

'Of course I'm not *afraid*,' snapped Jess.

'It's a treasure hunt,' explained Paddy. 'We have to find the treasure, it's lost somewhere in the dungeons.'

'Who told you that?'

'M-Marcel. Rachel, Lili, Jean-Claude. They all told me.'

'It's true,' said Jean-Luc. 'Their treasure is lost.'

Jess remembered that French people go in for organized games. At any big campsite there would be a team of young men and women like Jean-Luc, who ran volley-ball tournaments and took the campers' children off on paper-chases and treasure hunts. It was part of being French. Probably the children were friendly. They were teasing and she was imagining things out of fear of foreigners. And she liked Jean-Luc a lot. Besides, she wasn't going to have some ratty-pigtailed French girl call her a coward.

'All right,' she said. 'Where do we look? Are there clues?'

No, one answered. 'This way,' urged Paddy. 'Come on!'

There was another narrow passage, in pitch darkness. At least this time there was a level floor and walls she could feel along. Still nobody switched on a torch. Jess couldn't believe they didn't have one. They were trying to scare her and Paddy: she was not going to give them the satisfaction of hearing her beg for a light. But why didn't Jean-Luc switch on *his* torch? He must have one! Who would lead children on an underground treasure hunt – if that was what it was – without one? Maybe the rotten children had stolen it. She was more and more sure that something had gone wrong with this game, it was getting out of hand. But she felt powerless. It was easier to go on than to try to call a halt. She kept hold of Paddy's arm, and fumbled along the wall, pausing every moment to check that her waist-pouch was still there. Hands tugged at her, and pinched her. The children whispered *this way*, and *take care*: but they giggled nastily, and the pinches hurt. A sly jerk at her ankle brought her to her knees on hard cold stone.

'Stop that!' she yelled.

Footsteps pattered. She'd lost her grip on her brother. 'Paddy? *Paddy!*'

She stood up. She couldn't reach the walls any longer. She groped and stumbled, nearly braining herself as she fell against rock. She was disoriented, didn't know which way to move. 'This is crazy,' she muttered.

Then there was light, but it didn't help. The children were running away. Their faces looked back: hollow-cheeked, painted with loss and fear and neglect. Their hard eyes glittered. She heard Jean-Luc calling his roll: Marcel, Simone, Liliane, Jean-Claude . . . But they were gone. They wouldn't come to him.

She saw Jean-Luc. He was crouched by the wall of the tunnel, shading his torch in his hands as if he was afraid to show its light, even here far underground.

'What's wrong?' she whispered, glad to see the torch but bewildered and astonished. She thought he was crying, but that couldn't be right . . .

'I have lost the treasure. They will not forgive me.'

'But it's a game, Jean-Luc. I thought it was a game. *I don't understand.*'

The dim light went out. The children's scuffling footsteps had faded into silence. Cold, lightless, utter silence.

Some kind of dizzy spell, thought Jess. She must've nearly knocked herself out, when she tripped over. She was on her knees. She seemed to be alone. She must have been left behind accidentally, Jean-Luc wouldn't play a trick like this. But those children might do anything. She groped in front of her, afraid there'd be a hole in the floor, or something nasty for her to step on. Her fingers found something soft and jerked away, returned, and discovered a soft bag with something hard-edged inside.

I bet this is their treasure, she thought. She put the bag

in her waist-pouch. She wasn't going to open it in the dark. There was probably something gruesome inside, if Marcel had anything to do with organizing this 'game'. Now how am I going to get out of here? she wondered. She was determined not to panic. She could *feel* the French children watching her. In a moment, a light would come on, and they'd all be laughing.

Jess waited, but nothing happened.

Silence.

She yelled. 'Paddy! PADDY!'

'Jess?'

He was there beside her. She grabbed him. He was solid, warm and breathing. For a moment, this was enough of a relief to make her delirious with joy.

'Shall I put my torch on now?' he asked, in a small voice.

Jess dropped the hug. She stared malevolently at where she imagined her little brother's face to be.

'You had a torch. *All this time?*'

'Yes. In my pack. Mum said to bring it, didn't you bring yours? It's still here.' He giggled. 'You can't eat torches.'

'I forgot mine. *Why didn't you get it out before?*'

'They weren't. So I couldn't. They'd have thought we were scared.' Jess's hands reached to strangle. But Paddy switched on his small torch, and she forgot about violent retribution.

They were crouching on a stone floor, in a small, perfectly round chamber. The walls went up like the walls of a chimney. There was no break in them, anywhere.

'*What?*' breathed Jess.

She got up and walked around: feeling the close-set stones and peering carefully at every crack. The floor was stone flags. None of them seemed to have been moved for hundreds of years.

There was no way in or out.

'It *can't be*!'

'There must be a secret passage,' said Paddy placidly.

Jess didn't remember coming through a doorway, or any sound of shifting stone. But he had to be right. She went round the walls again, and found nothing. She felt completely confused. She looked at Paddy. He'd lost his hairband-eyepatch, and the feathers; his warpaint stripes were faint smears. He was happy enough now. How long before the batteries ran out?

'There's a trick to getting out, of course. We'll find it.'

'I wish I had something to eat,' sighed Paddy. 'They ate all my chocolate.' He laughed. He looked at Jess uncertainly.

For a moment Jess considered the awful possibility that the French children had led Paddy and her in here, left by a secret exit and just *gone home*, abandoning the English to their fate. What if it were true? What if she and Paddy were trapped in a doorless dungeon with no food or water and no one who knew where they were. . . ? Suddenly, she gasped. 'Paddy! Shine your torch up!' He shone the beam around the walls.

'NO! Straight up!'

It was there, high up in the blackness: the shadow of a criss-cross grille.

'I know where we are!' she cried. 'It's that place by the lift! The place I said was probably an old well.'

It was not a well. The tour guide had explained that the covered pit in the undercroft was 'the legendary oubliette-pit,' which was supposed to have been built to imprison a bishop who had offended the local gentry, a few hundred years ago. According to the legend, the bishop had been kept in it for twenty years, his food and water lowered to him by ropes. The tour guide had said there was no proof of the story, and nobody actually knew what the dry well was for. Jess, after her short reluctant tour of the *real* dungeons of Rochers-Jumeaux, was convinced that every evil story told about this place was true – and worse. But she didn't care about that now.

'It's dark up there, but there must be someone about: they're having a reception in the state apartments. Paddy, *yell*!'

'Help!' they shouted. 'HELP!' And then, because only French people would be listening: 'M'AIDEZ, M'AIDEZ!'

MAYDAY, MAYDAY, like a ship in distress . . . They yelled until their throats were sore. At last, light sprang on them from above. There were voices. They saw faces peering down.

It took time before they were rescued. Someone had to go and fetch a caretaker, and he had to fetch a strange basket-thing and fasten it on to a rope winch: this was the contraption that the castle staff used when they went down to clean the stonework and clear up the rubbish that tourists poked through the grille.

It was lucky for Jess and Paddy that a tour of the château had been part of the programme for the civic reception. If not they'd have been in trouble, because every year after the end of the *son et lumière*, the castle was closed for a week. They would not have found a way out. As far as the caretaker knew, there was no secret passage. All this Jess learned when she and Paddy had been lifted to safety, and were standing in a crowd of elderly men and women, all in formal evening dress. The working of the winch was explained in detail, and the castle's cleaning routine, and the terrible danger they'd been in.

'Who put you down there? Where are the friends who did this? They are imbeciles!'

'Who is responsible? Where are your parents?'

Jess felt dreadful when the people started demanding. *where are your parents?* She was afraid there'd be a fine for trespassing, some awful large sum of money. The whole holiday would be ruined. Paddy seemed far more scared than when they were trapped in a doorless dungeon. Jess didn't know what was wrong with him, until he whispered: *'Are they fairies? Have we got into fairyland?'* He stayed silent and big-eyed, clinging to Jess, staring at the jewels and glittering evening dresses.

She pretended she couldn't speak French at all – and very fortunately, none of the important guests spoke fluent English. Or if they did, they kept quiet about it. The caretaker was angry, but the guests wanted to get back to their reception, and Paddy was being petted by the jewel-bedecked old ladies. Maybe these kind women had something to do with it, Jess lost track of the French talk. But miraculously, they were dismissed with a caution.

The caretaker took them solemnly to the main gate, through doors that he unlocked with a lot of annoyed jangling of keys. He walked them back to the party, using a paved footpath they hadn't known about, that twisted down and around the base of the crag. The fireworks were over but the disco was blaring and the fun was still in full swing. Mum and Adam had just gone off to hunt for Jess and Paddy, but Dad was where they had left him. The man made a long grumbling complaint about disorderly foreign children. But he stalked away, to Jess's deep relief, without mentioning money.

'Did he say you were *inside* the castle?' Dad was bemused.

'We were lost,' explained Jess. 'Well, we weren't really lost. But *he* thought we were.'

'We were in the dungeons!' piped up Paddy.

Jess pinched him. 'We were *pretending* that we were in

the dungeons. We were playing with some French children.'

Dad and Mum hadn't been really worried. They'd assumed the two younger Ravens had gone back to the disco. Mum and Adam came back. Jess explained again about playing with local children and getting caught by the officious caretaker. This time Paddy had enough sense to keep his mouth shut.


The storm that had been threatening must have known it was expected to bring the celebrations to a spectacular end, in torrents and thunder. It held off until morning. Jess woke early. She put her nose out into grey daylight and found rain falling like tent-pegs: slam, slam, slam on the five-star refugees. She groaned and started to strip her tent, prepared for the grim chore of striking camp in the wet.

While she was packing up she found her waist-pouch, and remembered the children's treasure. She took it out. It was a bag made of worn green and red brocade, like a piece cut from an old curtain. It wasn't very big. There was something like a hard, shallow box inside: maybe a tobacco tin? She turned it over in her hands. 'Jean-Luc,' she murmured.

She wondered what the treasure was. Jean-Luc might be looking for this today. It would be nice to see him again . . . She began to loosen the cord.

*Darkness. A cold, foul-smelling darkness. Somewhere, a child was screaming. The children were screaming in words she didn't understand. Something terrible, terrible . . .*

'Stop it!' cried Jess. 'Stop it.'

The darkness was gone. She was kneeling in the blue tent. The brocade bag was lying where she had thrown it, in that moment of strange panic . . . Jess picked it up.

'Stupid . . .' she muttered. 'I don't know what came over me.' But her heart was thumping.

She wanted to throw it away. Throw it away, forget the whole thing . . . But this was her only connection with Jean-Luc. She stared at the bag for a moment, then abruptly stuffed it in the bottom of her rucksack. She could leave Jean-Luc a note at the office.

Packing up didn't take as long as Jess had thought it would, because this year there was only one tent. Mum and Dad decided it would be more fun to get out of Rochers and have breakfast in a bar somewhere down the road. The Silver Slug was far away before Jess remembered the note she'd meant to write – and realized she hadn't even told Jean-Luc that her family was staying at the campsite. So that was that. There was nothing she could do. The 'treasure' was hers, and she would never see Jean-Luc again.


Paddy was six. After a day or two he'd gone on to new adventures. He didn't mention the dungeon treasure-hunt or the nasty children again. But Jess remembered uncomfortable details: the stone room with no exit. The cruelty of those children, in their ragged clothes that belonged to no particular time or place . . . She was confused, because Jean-Luc had seemed so normal, and she had truly liked him. But she had thoughts she didn't like at all. She was sorry she'd accidentally walked off with the treasure, but she felt – the way she'd felt in the castle courtyard the afternoon before the party – that she had had some kind of lucky escape.

From what? She would rather not say. Not even to herself.

★

The weather turned blissfully hot and clear on the last day before the drive to the overnight ferry. They had camped in an orchard on the edge of a cathedral city. It was quiet, because the French holidays were over. Swallows flitted under the apple branches. There was a stream where turquoise winged dragonflies played over the shallows. Adam told Paddy these insects were French fairies and he ought to call them *Melusine*. But Paddy said, no, French fairies are fat and they have earrings and long dresses.

They went for a walk, the three of them, along a dusty harvest-time lane. Adam was in his chair. He'd been using it most days since Rochers. They climbed (the wheelchair humming merrily) to the top of a hill, and found a viewpoint, with picnic tables. Jess stretched herself out on a bench and gazed at the sky. It was the golden end of summer and soon they'd be in England again: back to school, boring things. Her eyes closed.

She sat up. Had someone called her name?

The children were gathered round her bench. They were looking at her with hungry eyes. '*Have you got it?*' asked one. She had forgotten the names in Jean-Luc's roll. Was that Marcel? They pressed closer. She could smell their unwashed bodies, she could see the gaps in their teeth. Their hands were like claws, reaching out to drag her away with them into the dark. And there was Jean-Luc. He was smiling, but as desperate as the children themselves.

'Excuse me,' he said. 'You must have it, surely? Please!' He looked so frightened. 'Please!' he cried again.

Jess woke, with a startled jolt. Paddy was playing at the edge of the golden stubble with his police car and his batmobile. *Vrrm, vrrm, crash crash crash.*

'Was I asleep?'

'Snoring,' said Adam cheerfully. 'Time to go back.'

There were no children. She jumped up and ran to the lane. It was empty as far as you could see in both directions. Adam came out behind her.

'What's up, Jess?'

'Nothing,' she said. 'It's weird. I didn't know I was dreaming.' She shook her head, shaking away the too-real memory of those voices, those hungry eyes. 'I'll be glad to be home. I'm tired of France.'

# Three

AUTUMN TERM BEGAN. THE FRENCH COUNTRYSIDE was a million miles away. Adam was doing 'A' levels at college, like any other eighteen-year-old. But he was definitely sicker. He tired easily, he used the chair more often. Mum and Dad – Mum was a programmer and Dad was a machine tool setter – were both working part-time, so they could be with him as much possible. That meant not much money for a family of five, even with the help they were given for Adam's special expenses, like the chair and the holiday loan of the Silver Slug. But her parents didn't look on it as a sacrifice, Jess knew that, and neither did she. She understood that Mum and Dad were hungry for Adam. They wanted to be with him the way you would feel if you were in love with someone, and the time was coming when you would never see them again. And yet life went on, the same as ever: the routine of school and home and school.

One afternoon they had sex education last thing. Some kids tried to embarrass the teacher, and failed. Some embarrassed themselves by asking really ignorant questions. These were boys, inevitably. Boys never know when to keep their heads down. But nobody laughed too much, because Jess's class were fairly kind-hearted. And then the little bit about Aids sobered everybody. Afterwards Jess walked to the tube with her friend Noelle. As they stood on the platform, Noelle pinched Jess's arm.

'Cheer up. You haven't got it. You've never been with a boy, I know that. And you'd never do drugs.'

Jess realized she hadn't said a word since they walked out of the classroom.

'It's not *that*. I was thinking of something else.'

'Well, dump it then. Come on, tell. I don't like to see you miserable.'

Noelle had never 'been with a boy' either, as Jess knew. Her parents were very strict. If they'd been slack it would have been the same. Noelle had made up her own mind not to mess about.

They were so different to look at, these two, that it was comical: Jess so pale, Noelle so dark. They didn't care. They had met one day in first year, and each had recognized in the other the same determination. Their school was as good as it could manage to be. It was a place you could be proud of, considering the state of some inner-city comprehensives. But there were always temptations. Noelle and Jess had made up their minds to succeed, even if it meant not being 'cool', or whatever. They had their eyes on the prize. Noelle was going to be an architect. Jess, of course, was going to discover the cure for Sales' Myasthenia.

They climbed on to the train. 'Is it bad news?' asked Noelle gently 'Have things, you know, got worse?' She knew about Adam.

Jess shook her head. 'I'm just tired. I don't want to talk.'

The train stopped. It started again, and crawled to the next station. It stood for ages, then the doors opened and a voice said: 'Owing to, . . . blah blah blah . . . terminates here . . .'

'Bomb scare,' groaned Noelle.

They followed the movement of the crowd that got off their train, and met some other people from school . . . who didn't know anything useful. Finally the speaker system told everyone this station was CLOSED, and they were herded out on to the street.

'I'm going to get a bus,' said Noelle. 'If they're running.'

'I'll walk to Liverpool Street,' decided Jess. It was where she usually changed trains. 'And get the overground. If it's running.'


Sex education meant something to Jess, that most thirteen-year-olds didn't dream of. She had to decide, in a few years' time, if she would take the test that showed whether she was a carrier of Sales' Myasthenia. And then, if she was a carrier, she had to decide what to do about it, if she wanted to have a family.

Jess's mum said that if she'd known she would never have had children. But how could you match that with how much she loved Adam, and Jess, and Paddy? Jess's grandmother, Dad's mum, said you shouldn't try to find out. You should leave it to God. Jess could see the attraction of that. But poor God! There was so much wrong with the world. So many wars, and millions of refugees dying of starvation, terrorists casually murdering people they didn't know. And it seemed as if what was wrong couldn't be fixed, because whatever people tried they only made things worse.

Jess thought maybe this was the only kind of world you

could have. It was this, with all the horrible things, or NOTHING . . . God had probably invented human beings just to have a shoulder to cry on, because Creation was such a mess and it was never going to get better. Poor God, it seemed a rotten trick to hand the choices back: *You deal with this, I can't cope.*

She plodded through the drab streets, her mind caught in a bad spiral that was taking her down into a real depression. It was a day at the beginning of October, fresh and chill after weeks of muggy dull greyness. The air was sharp, with a touch of early frost. Trees growing out of the pavement had golden and russet leaves. A virginia creeper blazed scarlet on a warehouse wall, the clear sky was turning a deeper blue as sunset drew near. Jess didn't notice. She just walked. Finally, she did notice that the street was strangely quiet. There were no other passers-by. There was no movement in or out of shops and offices.

She stopped and looked up and down. It was eerie. There was literally no one about. She grimaced and walked on resignedly. *Bomb scare! Bomb scare!* She was sure she knew what had happened. She'd run into a police action. The road must be closed ahead. She expected to find yellow-jackets and bollards and tape blocking her way, when she turned the next corner.

The next street was just as quiet.

Jessica groaned again. How stupid, she said to herself. I'm *lost*. There was no one about, because somewhere she'd turned off the busy thoroughfares that lead to the big station. She was in a backwater, a patch of London that had fallen asleep on its feet: and she had no idea just where she was on the map. She looked around for a street-name and couldn't see one. She pulled out her *A to Z*. Though she'd lived in London all her life she wasn't too proud to carry a street guide. She looked for somewhere to sit down and consult it.

The street was lined with shabby warehouses and derelict-looking office buildings. Narrow doorways full of dust were plastered with little metal plates, belonging to firms that seemed to have gone out of business years ago. On the corner opposite her a pair of tall yard doors stood open, showing a glimpse of ancient cobbles; and a whitewashed building that could have been a stable for dray horses. Beside Jess there was the entrance to a little park. She pushed the wrought-iron gates, and stepped inside.

She walked into a well-tended garden. It was quiet, even more quiet than the street outside: and pretty. It was hard to believe that grimy London was only a step away. The flowerbeds were laid out in a formal pattern. In the centre there was a tiny chapel – a doll's house church with a miniature spire. A row of big rusty horse-chestnut trees blocked off the view beyond. On either side, the garden was flanked by bare dingy walls. She noticed a soft sound. On each side of the path she had chosen, there was a fountain set among the flowerbeds. She walked to the left-hand one, and sat down on a green-painted bench. In the middle of a circle of raked gravel, the water rose in a modest jet of silver from a round pool; and fell back with an endless murmur. She could see the chapel, and the chestnut trees. She like the way the trees broke up the view. It looked as if the garden could go on for ever in that direction, like something in a fairytale.

This reminds me of somewhere, thought Jess. She couldn't capture the memory. But there was something magical about the place. The whisper of the fountain soothed her. She could almost fall asleep.

A figure crossed along the end of the path opposite her bench: stopped, turned, and began to come her way. Jess stood up, suddenly alarmed. While it was empty the garden was magical. A strange man made it threatening.

But he halted before he reached her, looking as unsure as Jess felt.

'Hallo? Excuse me, but don't I know you?'

He spoke English, with a French accent. For a moment she didn't know *where* she recognized him from. Then she remembered.

'Jean-Luc!,' she exclaimed 'You *are* Jean-Luc!'

'And you are Jessica.' He grinned, the shy way she remembered. He looked exactly the same, except that his tan had maybe faded.

'But what are you doing in London?'

'Oh . . .' He shrugged. 'Perhaps I came to meet you.'

She thought that was an odd sort of answer – very French!

He looked around at the garden. 'I found this place when I was last in England,' he told her. 'I suppose I came back because it is so pretty, and peaceful.'

He's only Adam's age, thought Jess, and he sounds as if he's been to England lots of times. She was impressed. 'What a coincidence. I've never been here before. I was trying to get to Liverpool Street station: I think I got lost.'

'You are lost? Maybe I can help you –'

They laughed, because Jessica was supposed to be the native, and Jean-Luc the tourist here. They sat down on the bench, and Jess opened her *A to Z*. But she didn't want him to tell her the way to get to Liverpool Street. There must be something better they could do with this meeting, if only she knew how to begin.

Jean-Luc seemed to feel the same. 'It's quite simple,' he said. He found the page and pointed . . . But he laid the book down.

'It's so good to see you, Jessy, and so mysterious! I never thought you would appear again!'

*Jessi!* he said: making her name sound strange. She longed to find out more about him.

'Are you a student? Are you at college in London?'

'Me?' He looked surprised. 'It's a long time since I was a student.'

'Oh,' said Jess. She was mortified, because she was in her uniform. She'd thought Jean-Luc was about seventeen when she met him that night in France. He couldn't be *that* old. But she must look horribly young. She never bothered with make-up for school, though you were allowed a bit. White eyebrows, pig's eyelashes, school shirt and skirt, arrgh.

They chatted, or tried to chat. It was a failure. They managed, like pitifully poor tennis players, to knock two or three sentences to and fro. Then the ball dropped again and they both sat silent, full of helpless friendly intentions.

'Jessica: it's a pretty name.'

'No one calls me Jessica. I'm always Jess. No one calls me 'Jessy' either . . . But you can, if you like. It sounds nice.'

He smiled. But his shy, polite expression reminded her of the night when they had met in France: and that reminded her of Adam, and everything. It was no use, she could not invent casual things to say.

'I need someone to talk to!' she burst out.

She could not talk to Noelle. She had told Noelle too much about Adam being ill, and how miserable it was. All that stuff was still there in Noelle's kind, pitying eyes, when Jess wanted to forget and be normal. It became impossible to escape. Her troubles were with her all the time, in everything she touched.

Jess was one of those lucky people who do not blush easily. She just sat rigid, horrified that she'd cried out like that. But Jean-Luc was not embarrassed. He nodded, with grim sympathy.

'So do I,' he said. 'I also need someone who knows

nothing, to be my . . . confidante. Perhaps that's why we have met, you and I. Shall we walk?'

They walked through the garden, following the neat paths. The city of London was all around them, but Jess didn't hear the hum of traffic. No one else came in to walk, or to sit on one of the green-painted benches with the scrolled iron legs and arms. The only sound was the delicate whisper of the fountains.

'I know what this place reminds me of,' she said. 'It's like a French place. Very precise and –' (she sought for a way to express this unmistakeable quality, without making it an insult) '– sure of itself.'

Jean-Luc nodded. 'Yes, true: it is a French garden.' *Bien sûr* he said. Jess grinned to herself, because a rough translation of that expression sounded funny to a Londoner. *Well* sure of itself. Yes: Frenchness was like that. She kicked up gravel with the toe of her boot. 'It's Adam, you see. My brother. He's sick. He's only eighteen and he's *dying*. And I love him so much. He's years older than me but he never ignored me. He was always my friend, my protector. I looked up to him, he was fun, but I felt so safe . . . Even up to last year, it was still the same between us. But it's not even that he's dying. That *hurts* but what's so bad is the day to day horribleness, the way *it never goes away*. And no one thinks of what it means to me. Mum and Dad look at me as if they can't remember my name . . .'

As Jess poured out her heart Jean-Luc said nothing, he simply walked beside her. But his silence was more comforting than words. She felt that he was not secretly thinking – the way other people, even Noelle, were always thinking, when they listened and sympathized – *glad its not me*.

They came to the chapel. Jess assumed it would be locked. But the doors in the neatly-swept porch opened at a touch. Inside there were benches, facing an altar that was canopied with white stone tracery. Coloured light fell through the pointed windows. There was a smell of floor polish.

'How old is Adam?'

'He's eighteen.'

'Do you think, it was because he was ill that he remained your companion? Might he not have grown away from you years ago, otherwise?'

Jess scowled. 'Are you telling me I should be glad that he's sick? That it's spiritual and uplifting? I hate that sort of talk.'

'No,' answered Jean-Luc calmly. 'I am saying, the good things and the bad things in life are more closely woven together than you think. I'm not saying this itself is good or bad. I only make the observation.'

'Then there's Paddy,' said Jess. '*He won't leave me alone*. He's my other brother, he's six. I look after him, because Mum and Dad are preoccupied with Adam. Of course we can never do what I want, because he's only a little boy. I have to do what he wants. Play with him: play ludo, play pirates, whatever he likes. As if there aren't other little kids he could play with.'

'So, you have become for Paddy the good companion that Adam has before been for you?'

Jess's eyes stung. She folded her arms over her briefcase, hugging it like armour. She was embarrassed. She shouldn't have started complaining about Paddy, that was petty. Now Jean-Luc's gentle comment had made her want to cry. 'I suppose so,' she muttered. Jean-Luc tactfully pretended to be examining the memorial tablets on the chapel walls, though it was too gloomy for anyone to read, in here. There must be a light switch somewhere. Neither of them suggested hunting for it.

'Was there a history of the disease? In your mother's family?'

'Nothing, not so far as anyone can tell. It's a . . .'

'A random mutation.'

'That's right. This kind of myasthenia, it can be either. It didn't have a name until fifteen years ago, when a doctor called Sales put some odd cases of wasting disease together, and decided there was a common cause.'

'Yes,' said Jean-Luc.

'It's genetic, she told him. 'They've found the defective gene that causes it. It codes for something vital in the sheath of your motor nerve fibres: codes, that means DNA code, you know.'

'I know.'

'But finding the defective gene doesn't mean there's a cure. People think it does, but it doesn't. They might *never* find out how to fix it . . . Girls don't get sick. They have a one in something – I forget what – chance of getting off free. If they're unlucky, they're carriers and nearly all their boy children get sick and die before they're twenty-five. Paddy's okay. I have to decide whether to take a test and find out. What would you do, if you were me?'

He didn't answer. She waited, and realized that he wasn't going to. He was right. Only Jess could answer that one. She stood staring at the altar, aware of Jean-Luc somewhere behind her, sitting on one of the benches.

'This place reminds me of the chapel at the château, at Rochers. It's really nothing like, but I don't often go into churches . . .' In the dim light, stained by coloured glass, the memory of that brief 'vision' of hers returned to her with strange vividness. She saw again the spiked circlet of jewel colours, hanging in dark air.

'Do you live there? In Rochers, I mean.'

'My home is nearby.'

'You know the "Virgin of the Chaplet"?'

'I know it.'

'Something strange happened to me. I was looking at that statue and suddenly *wham*, the jewelled crown in her hands came to life. It was like something alive, but woven out of jewels, there's no other way I can describe it. I suppose it was a trick of the light but, wow, it was *so beautiful*: and so *clear*. I can remember every detail. I think I'll never forget –'

'*La couronne*,' murmured the voice behind her. 'I have had moments like that. A little like. The mind works so. It is a living cloud that forms and reforms, taking shape and creating pattern from chaos. It is a fortune-teller's crystal ball, in which scraps of images gather. Suddenly you glimpse the whole picture, for an instant, and then it is gone.'

'I thought, maybe what I saw was the original. The mediaeval one with the real jewels, that was lost. Kind of a ghostly message . . .' She laughed. 'That sounds stupid, I don't really believe it – and anyway why me? Why should I have a vision of the lost treasure of Rochers?'

'I don't know,' said Jean-Luc softly. 'I don't know.'

His voice sounded strange. She wished she hadn't started talking about Rochers. Almost unconsciously, she'd decided that she wasn't going to ask questions about their first meeting: about the horrible children, or the practical joke they'd played on two tourists. He could explain everything, she was sure of that. She just felt she'd rather not go into it . . . Now she'd broken her own resolve. Oh no. Why did she have to mention the word 'treasure', reminding them both of that nasty game? She knew she'd done something fatal. She looked around.

'Jean-Luc?'

Oh no. The chapel was empty.

He wasn't in sight when she got outside. She walked away from the garden without looking back, furious with herself. An amazing coincidence had happened to her, and she'd wasted it. He'd taken offence, or been embarrassed, because she'd reminded him of those horrible children: and now he was gone.

It was pathetic. She'd been so nervous, she'd asked him no sensible questions. She didn't know where he was staying, or how long he was in London. She hadn't told him her address, or anything. She couldn't even remember which language they had been speaking: probably a hotchpotch mixture of both. But they'd been getting on so well. What a shame!

She found her way to Liverpool Street easily, and caught a train at once. It was Adam's day to see his physiotherapist at the hospital. Dad had gone to pick him up from college and take him. When Jess got in, Mum was furiously scrubbing the worktops in the kitchen. She looked up, struggling to register Jess's presence.

'Are you late?'

'Probably. There was a bomb scare or something on the tube.'

Mum wiped straggles of hair off her face with the back of her rubber glove. Her eyes focused on her daughter.

'You look tired. Poor Jess, it's a rotten journey. But it's the best school we could get you into . . . I wish it was better.'

Jess's heart melted. Poor Mum, scrubbing counters to try and stop herself thinking. She'd taken to housework in a big way since Adam started getting sicker. She said it was good therapy.

'I *like* my school,' she said. 'Don't worry about me, Mum. I'm fine. Really I am.'

She didn't know it was going to happen, but she found herself walking into a hug. They held each other, wordless, wrapped in the stinging smell of bleach: then came apart, Mum smiling ruefully.

'I've had enough drudge-therapy. I'll make us a cup of tea.'

Falling asleep that night, Jess thought about Jean-Luc. How old was he? He could be nineteen. If he was nineteen there wasn't *too* much of a gap, and everyone said Jess was very mature. But if he was twenty? Or more? No, that was too old . . . She pulled a face into the pillow, she knew these calculations were daft. She'd only talked to him twice, and almost certainly they would never meet again. But she thought about how nice he'd been, and how much better she could have managed their conversation. She realized before she fell asleep that – though the bad stuff was still there – her horrible depression had vanished. Jean-Luc had swept it away. What a pity she would never see him again.


That was Monday. On Wednesday Jessica was woken by a hideous banging and tremendous snarling noises. She opened her eyes and saw the wall by the door of her room shaking. As she watched, horrified, a chunk of plaster came free and jerked into the air, tearing a flap of her wallpaper with it.

'Dad!' she screamed. 'What are you *doing*?'

She leapt out of bed and flung open the door. He was drilling holes in the wall, with a mess of wires round his feet.

'Just drilling out a channel for the cable,' he explained, pushing his goggles back on to the top of his head. 'I'm wiring up some more powerpoints, and speakers, for Adam's room.'

'But it's seven in the morning! And look at this!'

She dragged him in and showed him the mess.

'It's only plaster. I'll make it good.'

'You WON'T,' yelled Jessica. 'I DON'T WANT YOU IN HERE. I'll fix it myself!'

Her father stared at her as if he really couldn't see what was wrong. Dad never stopped working on things to make life easier for Adam. He'd even tinkered with an old joystick, so that Adam could still play shoot-em-ups now that his hands were getting weak and unreliable. He sometimes said he could make a fortune if he got one of these tricks of his into production. But he didn't have time for that. It was all for Adam.

He usually got up early. He couldn't sleep, he said. Bashing the house apart at seven in the morning was Dad's way of coping.

'Why are you always MESSING with things?' Jess kicked at the coil of cable. 'I live here too! I hate this!'

At last her father reacted. 'Now look here, young lady,' he bellowed. 'You don't talk to me like that . . . !'

'Chris –' called Mum, from downstairs. 'Jess? What's going on?' Paddy came out of the bathroom and stood wide-eyed. Adam's door stayed closed.

Mum came up and looked at them. 'Come down to breakfast.'

Jess left the house in a bitter state of misery. They didn't understand. She couldn't, in fairness, expect them to understand.

She managed to avoid Noelle at home time and rode on the tube alone. She got off at the station that had been closed by the bomb scare on Monday, and walked. She didn't know if she could remember the turns she'd taken in her misery that afternoon. But she tried, and soon she passed a scruffy sandwich bar that seemed familiar. She turned another corner, and there was the cobbled yard that seemed to belong to another era of London. There were the wrought-iron gates. She slipped inside. The garden was empty and silent as before. It was a grey afternoon this time. The air had a smoky scent, as if someone had been burning leaves.

She went to the fountain. It was ridiculous to expect Jean-Luc to be here. But if he had decided – after he walked out on her – that he wanted to see Jess again . . . Then he might have thought, as Jess had thought, of coming back to this garden. Same time, same place. It wasn't likely. But it was the only chance. There were words cut into the base of the waterjet. *From the fig tree learn its lesson*, she read. It sounded vaguely like something from the Bible, or Shakespeare, but what did it mean? What fig tree, what lesson? The lettering went on, but it was hidden by the leaves of a water plant. The spray hissed and sighed, dappling her face with cold, tiny drops.

Of course he wasn't here.

There was a sound behind her, like a muffled sob. She spun around. Jean-Luc was huddled on the green bench. He was turned sideways, away from her. His head was bowed, his brown hair flopped over his eyes. His hands were knotted between his knees.

'Jean-Luc? . . . Is it Jean-Luc?'

He must have come up while she was peering at the fountain, but he looked as if he'd been hunched like that for hours. He unfolded himself, raised his face and looked at her blankly, as if he'd forgotten all about meeting her here before. In one hand he was clutching a sheaf of paper, several sheets with scribbled drawing or writing on them. He let them fall.

'Jessica?'

He'd been wearing that loose dark jacket in August, and much the same clothes: a soft green shirt and battered khaki trousers. She remembered being pleased that he wasn't all chic and prissy, like some French boys. But now she stood and stared like an idiot, because his whole appearance was *strange*. It was more than the untidy clothes, or the fact that he was obviously miserable.

'You should not be with me here! Go away!' Then he looked suddenly puzzled. 'Did I call you? *Can* you leave?'

Jess made a decision. He had told her that he was in trouble too, that *he* needed someone he could talk to. She went to the bench and sat down beside him. 'I came back here because I hoped you'd think of coming. I wanted to see you again. You let me do the talking last time, now its your turn. What's wrong, Jean-Luc? You know you can tell me.'

'Wrong? Yes, terribly wrong. Who could do such a thing?'

'Do what?'

'People are capable of anything, when they are afraid. The greatest bravery, and the most shameful acts.'

'Jean-Luc, I don't understand. You'll have to explain.'

He turned away. She followed the direction of his eyes, and for a moment she saw *them*. They were hiding by the chapel. When they saw that Jess was there they ducked out of sight: but she'd seen enough to be sure. *Marcel, Simone, Liliane, Jean-Claude* . . . The children from the château. What on earth were they doing in London? This was stranger and stranger.

'Are you still looking after those children? Is it your job? Are you their teacher, or something?'

They were different ages, they couldn't be in one class. But in special schools, children of different ages are taught together. It was probably the same in France. She struggled to make sense of the situation. Jean-Luc was in charge of a group of special-needs children. He'd brought them to England on a school trip or something, and they were playing him up . . .

'No.' Jean-Luc sat up. He shook his hair out of his eyes, and spoke in a flat, neutral tone. 'I don't belong to any organisation. Yes, I was looking after the children. I have nothing more to tell you.'

'Okay, fine.' Jess was even more bewildered. She decided she couldn't cope with this. She stood up, about to walk away. But his expression changed. He smiled.

'Jessy. It is you, excuse me. I thought I was talking to someone else.' He stood up from the bench and moved a step or two – always with his eyes on the children's hiding place. 'I would not have brought you to this vile cell. But since you are with me, it's good to have a companion . . .'

Suddenly Jess was with him, in a small bare room. He came back to the bench: but it wasn't a bench any longer. They were sitting on a narrow iron bed, under the harsh yet dull light of a single naked electric bulb. Jean-Luc watched the door.

'How did you *do* that?' she breathed, amazed.

The room was as bare as a prison cell, and it had the feeling of a prison. The grey walls seemed to hold the echo of countless fearful voices: protesting, pleading innocence: sobbing and begging for mercy. But it was a refuge, from the cruelty of those children. Jess knew this, without knowing how she knew . . .

'I thought I could escape,' he whispered. 'But I can never escape them. I can never return to them what they have lost.'

'The treasure?'

'Yes. The stolen treasure. Oh, Jessy, be afraid. They are coming. *Ils sont terribles* . . .' He buried his face in his hands for a moment: then lifted it and looked at her. '*Have you got it?*'

The make-believe, or whatever it was, seemed to dissolve. The French garden returned. Jean-Luc's question reminded her sharply of the dream she'd had, when she fell asleep on that hilltop viewpoint, on the way home from Rochers. All at once she knew she'd had that dream, that *nightmare*, often since they got back from France, but forgotten it on waking. It was always the same: the nasty children of that night at the château were looking for her. They'd tracked her down and they wanted their treasure.

Jess thought she must be dreaming now. But it didn't feel like a dream. She struggled for a rational explanation. 'Oh, I know what it is. You're *acting*. You're rehearsing a part . . .'

The children, of course, had been acting in the *son et lumière*. Maybe they were from a drama school, and now they were doing a show in London. She looked for the scribbled papers she'd seen. But he'd put them away at some point: they'd vanished.

He was shaking his head.

'You're not actors.' She laughed. 'All right, I've guessed. It's a game, like *Dungeons and Dragons*. Like make-believe for grown-ups? The quest for the lost treasure, the battle between good and evil, the Forces of Light versus the Dark Lord, that sort of thing?'

'I have seen the triumph of the Dark Lord,' Jean-Luc whispered, turning his grey eyes towards her. 'That is true.'

They were in the bare room. The metal door (she hadn't noticed it was metal before) began to open, a crack and then a crack more. No light showed on the other side, there was instead a line of blackness. Jean-Luc watched it with an expression of steady, hopeless terror. There was a scratching sound, like the noise of many small fingernails scrabbling. Jean-Luc drew a sharp breath. Jess herself nearly wailed aloud in terror as the little claw-like hands appeared and started to grope the air: feeling for their prey. It was as if they were pushing the lid off a coffin and reaching up from the grave.

'They want what they have lost. Jessy, *please!*'


On the train, going home, she stared at her own reflection in the dirty window. She rubbed her eyes. Had she fallen asleep? She looked at her watch, suddenly worried. Wrapped up in Jean-Luc's make-believe, she had lost track of time. It was not much later than usual. It had felt like ages, but she couldn't have stayed in the garden very long at all.

She could not believe that what had happened had been as strange as it seemed. It was a game, and Jean-Luc was very good at it . . . that was all.

It was amazing, what he'd been able to do with just a couple of gestures, a few muttered words. He'd made the 'police cell' seem completely real. She could see it now: the hatch in the door, for someone to look in and check you hadn't killed yourself. The blue-grey paint on the metal, lumpy over the hinges and looking as if it was coated in grease. She could remember the feel of the blanket on the cot. It was like a piece of grey cardboard.

She still wasn't sure exactly what had been going on. Jean-Luc had to recover 'the lost treasure'. He kept getting chased and caught, and escaping only to be caught again. The bad guys, those nasty children, represented ultimate evil, or something like that: and Jess was his faithful companion. It sounded totally childish. But it had been exciting. Jess hadn't played make-believe – except when she was doing it to humour Paddy, which didn't count – since she was little. She'd forgotten how much fun it was, how real it could seem. Jean-Luc had just pulled her in, no explanations, as if they'd been friends for years. Playing make-believe had made him seem younger too. She realized that on Monday, though it had been nice, it had been like talking to a sympathetic adult. Today he'd been more like the boy she'd met in France.

But the children . . .

In the grimy train window, the reflection of Jess's face crumped into a frown. Had she actually seen them? Or had that been her imagination getting carried away? She wasn't sure. When she thought of them she was uncomfortable. They didn't fit in with the idea that she and Jean-Luc had been caught up in a fantasy game. The part they played, if they were real, was too strange . . .

*Ils sont terribles.* They are terrible.

She didn't want to think about it. She'd seen Jean-Luc again, that was the important thing. And they were friends.


She wasn't late home. Not late enough for anyone to notice, anyhow. She watched television, while Paddy played with his pirates and his space-police around her feet, until it was time to eat. Over the shepherd's pie and carrots she got into an argument with her father, about recycling. Jess had to watch her family. They would generate ten times more rubbish than necessary, if she didn't keep on at them. Adam ate slowly. Jess could see Mum itching to help him. But she did not. Dad would be thinking of an electric-assisted knife and fork, that could be handled with strengthless hands. It was another day in the life, just another day.

After tea she went upstairs. There was more plaster hanging off her wall. She tore the chunks away and threw them in her bin. Then she tugged out the long hook from behind the chest of drawers on the landing, and pulled down the loft ladder.

'I'm going up in the loft,' she yelled. *'Don't put the ladder away*. I won't be long.'

'Can I come?' shouted Paddy from below.

'No you can't. Mum, Adam: *don't let him come after me.'*

She switched on the light. The loft was a junk heap. Dad and Mum talked about converting the loft into another room, if they ever had the money. Jess couldn't see it. There was so much *stuff* here, and nowhere else it could go. She fought her way through the boxes of forgotten bric-a-brac, the binliners full of old clothes, the rolls of left-over wallpaper. The last person to come looking for something up here had made a terrible mess – probably Dad: Mum was a tidy person. Finally Jess discovered the camping gear.

She found her own rucksack with no trouble. It was blue, with yellow flashes: nicely battered, but not too old. At the bottom, under the main bag, there was a compartment for stowing boots or wet gear. Since Jess never used it for anything important, it was a good place for things to lie forgotten. She knew that on the morning they left Rochers, she had stuffed the nasty children's treasure bag in there.

She'd forgotten about it. Or if she hadn't forgotten, she'd put it out of her mind. She'd never told Mum or Dad about the game in the dark under the château: never even thought of telling Adam. There was nothing to tell. If the treasure was valuable, what could she do? She didn't know the children's second names or anything else about them. She frowned, the rucksack felt light. But the treasure had been light. She groped in the bottom compartment. It was empty.

She tipped the rucksack upside down, searched every

pocket. She found a French ice-lolly wrapper, twenty centimes and two worthless bent tent-pegs. She sat back on her heels. The piles of junk cast black shadows in the light of the unshaded bulb.

'It's got to be here somewhere.'

She searched the rest of the camping gear, working doggedly through the heap of cooking-pans, collapsible bucket, gas stove, tent roll, sleeping bags, right down to the dusty boards that covered the loft's insulation matting. Nothing. There was no sign of the brocade drawstring bag that she had picked up in the darkness and examined briefly in her blue tent, that morning when the rain was beating down.

She remembered the thickness of the material, the colour of the tightly-bunched cord at the neck. It had once been red, but it had mostly faded to brown. She remembered feeling the outline of a box or a tin inside.

'It can't have just disappeared!'

It was cold up here. Under the château it had been cold too. The children's hands had been cold, when they touched and pinched and grabbed. Their fingers were like ice – although they'd just come, like Jess and Paddy, from a hot thundery August evening, outside. She remembered their faces, those young-old grimy faces with the sly, baleful eyes: and the way they gnawed at their chunks of black bread. They were good actors. You'd almost have thought they really *were* starving peasant-children, from the time of the Terror . . .

She remembered how frightened she had been, in her own tent the following morning, when she touched that bag. She was frightening herself again. Soon she'd be imagining that this familiar grungy loft was haunted by the ghosts of French children from the Terror: who had died hungry and cold, and hated anyone who was warm and fed . . .

A real child's clear voice came up from the bathroom.

'Adam!' yelled Paddy. 'A-Adam! My bathwater smells funny!'

'That's because you are sitting in it, my smelly sibling.'

That broke the spell. Jess choked, and grinned. Brothers!

The ladder rattled. She spun around like a frightened cat. Dad's head had appeared in the hatchway.

'What are you doing? You've been up here for hours.'

'I wanted something I left in my rucksack. But it's gone.'

'No one's touched the camping gear since we got back. Have another look tomorrow,' he offered. 'Be systematic.'

Jess rubbed her arms. 'Yes, Daddy. Systematic. The way you always are when you're looking for something.'

'None of your cheek,' he said amiably. He didn't bear a grudge for the way she'd yelled at him in the morning. They all made allowances for each other. His head disappeared.

'Don't be long!'

She wasn't going to tell Dad. Her ideas were too scary and too silly. She'd die of embarrassment if she had to tell anyone. And there was Jean-Luc. Oh no, it was too ridiculous. He was real enough. She would ask him when they met again, just casually ask *what about those children*? and he'd explain.

She couldn't remember if they'd exactly agreed to meet there. But she was somehow sure that if she went back to the garden, she would find him.

# Four

WHEN SHE WOKE UP NEXT MORNING, JESS TOLD herself there was no mystery. The 'treasure' could have slipped out of her rucksack anywhere between Rochers and London. That was why she hardly used the bottom compartment, it wasn't secure. The bag couldn't be important, it was just a prop in a fantasy game. And it hadn't *vanished*, there was nothing eerie about its disappearance.

She met Jean-Luc that afternoon, and again she was drawn into his intense make-believe. This time they were in a castle. It was the Rochers castle of course, but not the way Jess had seen it in August. The tourney yard, where the staging had been, was thick with grass. The old animal pens were still occupying the site of the menagerie gardens. They were dark, tumbledown dens. He showed her a wide pit, full of nettles, where a baron of the time of English Henry Eight (as he said) used to keep brown bears . . . The massive walls that had held state apartments and armouries and museums, were roofless shells. Only the chapel wing, and the bridge over the gorge, were intact. Over all: over the ruins and the town below, loomed the Tour de Garde – that had been a ruin when Jess visited Rochers. Now it was whole, and inhabited by sleepless evil. Jean-Luc and Jess crouched in what had been the wolves' den, behind a veil of honeysuckle and brambles, hiding from the horror that stalked outside. They were hunting for the treasure of Rochers, the jewelled crown. 'It is so beautiful,' Jean-Luc whispered. '*La couronne* is so beautiful and so precious, it cannot be lost forever.'

'How do you know it's still here?' she breathed, getting into the spirit of things. 'It vanished in the Revolution, did someone hide it from the mob?'

'Sssh!' he hissed. '*They!* They are listening! They will destroy me, they will never leave me . . .'

Jess went home on the train still in a daze of perilous adventure, carrying with her the scent of honeysuckle and the sound of Jean-Luc's urgent, desperate voice: the look of terror in his eyes. '*You will help me, Jessy. You must help me!*'

She met him often, through October and November. She went to the garden after school whenever she could manage it. She told Noelle she'd found a better route home, and Noelle accepted the story – as far as Jess could tell. The game changed, but there were scenes that returned, with variations. There were times when Jean-Luc's powers of illusion faltered, and one setting would blur into another: there'd be some modern touch like a drive in a jeep, when they had started off in mediaeval times. Sometimes there were two lots of baddies – the evil in the Tour de Garde was different from the nasty children. Sometimes it was only '*they*'. There were times when she couldn't understand what was going on at all. But it was like walking into a kaleidoscope. Every mysterious shift was as fascinating as the last.

At school she worked as hard as usual, especially in Biology and Chemistry, her best subjects. In both she was well ahead of her year group. Mrs Cohen, the Biology teacher, understood Jess's drive, and told her how lucky she was that she had the ability to match. She gave Jess extra practical work and lent her books. Jess spent lunchtimes in the library studying, and copying complex diagrams for practice. One day, thinking of Jean-Luc, she started trying to draw the jewelled crown as she had seen it in her 'vision'. She realized what she was doing: stared at her sketch and then quickly scrumpled it. It was *make-believe*. She mustn't let Jean-Luc's game pursue her into the real world.

One day, when she arrived in the garden it was raining hard. She took shelter in the chapel porch: and there was Jean-Luc in his thin jacket, shabby trousers and green shirt. She shook her umbrella out and closed it.

'You must be freezing!'

'Jessy?'

He held out his hand. She took it.

'Where are we? What is it today?'

'This is my home,' he said. 'This is the river that runs by my parents' house, at the bottom of our garden.'

They were standing in warm sunlight on the pebble beach of a river, that ran clear and brown under willow trees.

A battered blue rowing boat was lying upside down on the pebbles. Jean-Luc had been trying to make it watertight. He showed Jess how to caulk the gaping seams, while he patched a hole. The sun was hot on her shoulders. She took off her shoes and socks and felt the warm pebbles shift under her toes.

This was make-believe of a gentler kind. There was no

quest, no pursuit, no role-play. Jean-Luc didn't mention the treasure or the children. He seemed carefree: and hardly older than Jess herself. He told her that his full name was Jean-Luc Batiste, which she'd never known before. His father was a doctor and his mother was a pharmacist, in a little town in the country near to Rochers. He had no brothers or sisters. But he had cousins, and they had good times together: fishing, swimming in the river, going for drives in his father's old-fashioned pony and trap.

Jess was a city dweller. It was strange to hear about a French country childhood. It was like stories from another age. She told him about the plan she'd made with Noelle. They were going to the Caribbean together when they were eighteen. They would work their way, and Noelle had relatives to visit. Jean-Luc had distant relations on one of the French islands. He said he'd love to go there – if this war didn't happen.

'What war?' asked Jess. Jean-Luc frowned at her, puzzled. 'The war, you know. Don't your parents talk about it?'

He told her he was going to be a doctor, and Jess said she was going to be a molecular biologist. She'd told him that before, but this time he had trouble understanding her. They settled for *biologist*, he could cope with that.

Then it was time to test their efforts. In the game, Jean-Luc was wearing shorts. Jess rolled her skirt up at her waist. They turned the boat right way up and waded, pulling it into the river.

It began to fill with water at once. But they didn't mind. They let it settle, grounded on the pebbles, while they sat on the beach with their feet in the stream. Waterskaters darted, a fish rose with a plop from a deep pool under the willows. I'm so happy, thought Jess. But Jean-Luc spoke first.

'Do you believe in evil, Jessy?'

'I know that terrible things happen,' she answered.

'Yes,' he agreed softly.

'But when people do wrong, they don't think of themselves as being *evil*.' She was thinking of the awful things said and felt, by herself and by Mum and Dad, since Adam was ill. 'There's usually a reason, maybe they're suffering themselves. It's hard not to lash out when you're hurt. That's how it is for ordinary people. I don't know about, you know, monsters. Psychopaths. I know I can't imagine how they feel inside. But I suppose they have some kind of human reason – twisted, somehow.'

Jean-Luc looked at her seriously.

'You are a good girl.'

She was offended. She didn't want him to treat her like a good little girl. 'My good companion,' he murmured. 'Where did you come from, Jessy? Why are you here?'

She felt a change. He took her hand, but he was not a boy anymore. It was the adult Jean-Luc with the haunted eyes who was looking at her now. The make-believe river, which had been absolutely real to Jess a moment ago, faded strangely. It did not disappear but the life and joy went out of it.

'They are here,' he whispered. 'Even here. My whole life is theirs. Nothing is untouched. Only you, Jessy. Only you . . .'

'Who are they?' she cried, though she knew he could only mean the children, the terrible ones. The grip on her hand became painful. Jean-Luc started up, pulling her to her feet.

The willow branches were shaking. A child in rags came out from between them. She stood in the river, shaking her matted hair. Blood was running from her mouth, she held out hands like claws. The clear water ran grey and red-streaked, there was a stink of chemicals and rotten meat.

'Quickly, Jessy. Go! You must escape them, you at least –'

And Jess was on the train again, going home.

When she got in they were waiting for her. Mum and Dad and Adam had an appointment at hospital with Mrs Naira, Adam's consultant, to talk about a new treatment. Jess was supposed to be looking after Paddy. But it was okay. She wasn't very late.

She played with Paddy for as long as she could stand it. Then she plugged him into the cartoons on tv and went into the kitchen to make his tea. What was going on in the French garden? If she and Jean-Luc were playing a fantasy game, why did he never *say so*? He drew her in, without explaining anything. It must look mad if anyone was watching: a young man and a schoolgirl playing together like children, mending an imaginary boat . . . Was he crazy? That would be a simple explanation. But if he was crazy then Jess was crazy too, because it was all *real*: and frightening. It was easy to get caught up in the romantic adventure side of it. When she looked back, she saw that the fear was the real thing. Fear, and something precious that had been lost . . .

What about this new treatment? *There is no cure*. They'd all had that beaten into their heads. Even Paddy knew that Adam was going to die. Could this new drug treatment prolong Adam's life by ten years? Five? Could the doctors *promise* that?

Between Adam and those strange games in the French garden, she thought her head was going to explode.

She was making Paddy his favourite tea. Baked beans, mashed potatoes, and grated cheese. She ought to force him to come in here and help. He was too good at treating his sister like a useful slave. But she couldn't be bothered. The potatoes were boiling. She'd tipped the beans into a bowl (he preferred them cold). She was standing at the kitchen counter, grating cheese. A hand crept into view. It groped over the counter, sneaking towards the bowl of beans. Under the brilliant white light of the kitchen's fluorescent tube, every detail stood out. It was a child's hand. The nails were filthy. There was an open sore, oozing yellow stuff, on the back of one finger.

Jess didn't yell. Shock closed her throat. She leapt back from the counter, making a noise like *uuuh*, as if she was going to be sick. She couldn't bear to look. She jerked her head around, it was like forcing a broken machine to turn. For a moment *the creature was there*, in the Ravens' kitchen. It looked at her with blank malevolent eyes. It looked like a child in ragged, grimy outsized clothes, but she knew *it was not a person*. Ghosts are not people. She heard herself making another horrible shapeless noise: *huuunh*. She flung herself at the hand on the counter, beating at it with the cheese grater. Smashing it, beating it –

'Jess?'

Paddy was standing in the kitchen door, looking worried. The ghost had gone. There were shards of grated cheese on the floor.

'What's the matter, did you cut yourself?'

She stared at the little boy. She was shaking. 'Go back and watch the tv.' She snatched the bowl of beans.

'Hey! What are you doing! Why are you throwing my beans away?'

'I accidentally dropped washing-up liquid in them. Sorry. You can have peas with ketchup. *Go back and watch the television. I don't want you in here.*'

She finished scraping the polluted food into the bin

and sat down on a stool, swallowing hard. Please God, she prayed. Whatever it was, imagination or what . . . Don't let that happen again.

She took Paddy's tea in to him. When he'd finished, she let him put on his favourite video. He came and sat on her knee, like an overgrown puppy, and they watched it together.

Mum and Dad and Adam got back after Paddy was in bed. They were quiet and sad. Mrs Naira seemed to have spent the whole time warning them that she wasn't promising any miracles. That was what Dad kept saying. *She's not promising any miracles.* If Jess was looking strange, nobody noticed. She went to bed at her usual time. But she couldn't sleep. She sat up and opened her window, in the hope that fresh air would help her to think. It was cold, and the greyed-out London darkness smelled of winter.

She remembered the heat and the heavy sky of that August night in France. When the fireworks shot up, suddenly you could see the piled thunder clouds: and then they were invisible again. In the floodlights of the *son et lumière*, the château up on its crag had looked crisp and small, like a harmless romantic castle in a fairytale. That was what the guides and the leaflets wanted tourists to believe. *Oh no, nobody was tortured, there was no massacre, we have no nasty ghosts here!*

Jess knew that was a lie. Oh yes, Rochers had its ghosts. The children she and Paddy had met that night were vengeful ghosts, and Jean-Luc was their prey. It sounded ridiculous. But she couldn't lie to herself any longer. The knowledge settled in her, bewildering and heavy: it was impossible, but it was true.

'He has nobody but me to help him,' she whispered aloud. 'And I don't know what to do!'

She noticed that she could hear faint sounds from the

room next door: zzp, zzp, zzp, chee, chee, chee . . . She listened for a while. At last she got up quietly and crept out on to the landing. There was a line of light under Adam's door. She knocked.

'Enter.'

Adam's room was sacred. It was more private than her parents' bedroom. She'd known ever since she was a toddler that this was FORBIDDEN TERRITORY, and that Adam's friendship and kindness depended on her STAYING OUT OF HERE UNLESS INVITED.

'Hallo. Can I talk to you about something?'

Adam was slouched in front of his desk, the adapted joystick in his fist: playing shoot-em-ups in the middle of the night like any normal eighteen-year-old. He looked up, and smiled.

'Thought you'd never ask. Come in.'

Apart from the handrails his room was the same as ever. Same Ansell Adams posters, same prints of old photographs of grim-faced American Indian chiefs: same stacked bookshelves and messy desk. The clock on his bedside table said two fifteen am.

'Why d'you say, *thought you'd never ask?*'

'Parents are blind. I'm not. Siddown.'

She sat on his bed. 'What d'you think about the new treatment?' she asked. 'Will it work?'

'Nope.' He exited the game and swivelled his chair around: an office chair, this one, adapted by Dad. He gave her a crooked grin. 'But I could be wrong. Okay. Tell me about the boy trouble.'

She shook her head. 'It's not –'

His grin widened. 'Not boy trouble? The way you've been mooning around? Are you sure?'

'All right,' she admitted. 'It's *sort of* boy trouble.'

She told him about Jean-Luc, the whole story: the treasure-hunt game that had ended with Jess and Paddy in the *oubliette*, the brocade bag that had vanished. The meetings in the French garden, and the vivid, frightening make-believe adventures that she and Jean-Luc shared.

She looked at her brother helplessly. 'I don't understand any of it, Adam. I think of explanations, and they seem to make sense, but nothing really fits. You see I think the children may be ghosts from the time of the French Revolution: the guardians, or something, of a treasure that was lost in the Terror. I know that sounds crazy, but . . . I think it's true. *But he's not.* He dresses in modern clothes, he knows about cars and planes and things. He's an ordinary person from a small French town, who I met on holiday. But . . .' She shivered, remembering. '*They're always the same clothes.* The same clothes he was wearing that night in August. That's one of the things I've tried not to notice . . .'

She drew a breath. 'The one thing I understand is that Jean-Luc is in trouble and he came to me for help, and I *don't know what to do.* If I could return the lost treasure, maybe that would free him. But if I had it, if that wasn't an illusion, either I've lost it or . . . or the children took it back, somehow. It's gone.'

She had nothing more to say. She waited, hopefully, for Adam's verdict. He was sick, but he *hadn't* changed. He was still the big brother she adored: who had always known what to do, whatever trouble Jess was in.

Adam rubbed clumsily at the bridge of his nose, frowning.

'You say you're meeting this French boy in a park, on your way home from school, and playing scary fantasy games with him. But I haven't noticed you getting home late. Are you bunking off to meet him?'

'No! It *is* strange. That's another of the . . . the things I've tried not to notice. I meet him and we have adventures that seem to go on a long time: it's make-believe but it seems *real*, to him and to me too. And then . . . I get the usual train, and come home.'

'At your usual time?'

'More or less. It's as if being with Jean-Luc hardly takes up time at all.'

'Very odd.'

'Well, what do you think? What can we *do*?'

Adam must have some kind of answer.

'Mmm,' he said. 'Have you tried varying your route?'

'*What*?'

'Come home from school a different way. Don't even go near that park. Set off for Wimbledon and double back, whatever you like . . . You see, the way you tell it, either you've been falling asleep on the tube and having vivid dreams about a boy you met in France. Or else, you *have* been meeting this Jean-Luc and he's been frightening you somehow. The answer's simple: you should stop seeing him. Whether he's real or not, a different route will probably shake the demon lover.'

Science books were scattered over Adam's bed. He was doing the same 'A' levels as Jess would choose. That's DNA code, she thought looking at an open page and recognizing a string of letters CCTGGCAGGT-CAACGGAT . . . It was because a vital instruction in that secret language of life was missing, that Adam was sick. He was studying the cause of his disease. A vice clutched her insides. She had so much to learn, and there was so little time. *He was dying*. How could she expect him to concentrate on her troubles?

'But what about Jean-Luc?' she pleaded.

Adam took off his pebble glasses. He leaned forward. Green eyes like her own searched her face.

'Jess, is there more? Something you haven't told me?'

'No.'

'No drugs, no hanky-panky? You're not trying to break it to me, in a weird roundabout way, that *you're* in bad trouble?'

'NO!'

'Okay. Well, then we can keep the parents out of it I guess. Try my suggestion, and see what happens.'

It was Jean-Luc who was in trouble. To Adam it was Jess who needed help. She wanted to protest: *we have to rescue him!* But she realized suddenly how her story must sound. If he took it seriously, either Jess was involved in a very strange-sounding friendship, or she was going loopy. And Adam, who had always been her protector, was ill and helpless. How horrible for him . . . She thought of the ghost in the kitchen. She mustn't tell him about that. If she did, he'd be sure she was going crazy.

'Plus, you should take a warm milky drink at bedtime.'

He was smiling. She managed to dredge up a smile in return.

'Right. Ovaltine it is. I'll start tomorrow.'

'Destroys all known forms of supernatural disturbance.' He reached over and tweaked her nose, the way he used to do when she was five. 'Don't worry. Those dreams are only in your head.'

She went back to her room and managed to sleep: and found herself walking with Jean-Luc under the chestnut trees behind the chapel.

'Courage,' he said, huddling the dark jacket around him. 'One can make courage for oneself. You can be brave, I can be brave. Anyone who chooses can be brave . . . up to a point.'

'Yes,' said Jessica, grimly. 'I know that.' But his anxiety worried her. 'This *is* a game, isn't it?' she asked. 'You know, you frighten me sometimes. You aren't in real danger, are you?'

'It was a game,' he answered, with a bleak smile. 'A cruel game that they played. It was hide and seek.'

'I thought it was a treasure hunt.'

Then she woke, in her own bed. Adam's wrong, she thought. It doesn't matter what trains I take. Jean-Luc can find me anywhere. And so can the terrible ones, the children.


After school, she went to the garden. It was a frosty afternoon. The chestnut trees were leafless. Their branches hung down despondently, curving up at the ends like mastodon tusks. The sky was a cold pale blue. As usual there was no sign of a gardener, but someone had swept the paths clean of dead leaves. The water plants around the fountain had died back and been cleared away. Jessica read the inscription on the stone base: but it was just as puzzling now that she could read it all. *From the fig tree learn its lesson. When its branches become supple and put out leaves, then you know that the summer is near . . . .* I wonder what it means, she thought.

He wasn't there. She'd always been afraid it would end like this. He would vanish the way he'd come into her life, and she would never know what had happened to him. Her dream companion, her beloved friend. It didn't matter that she was fourteen – nearly – and he was adult. In the worlds of the garden she was no age and every age; and for him it was the same. She was Jessy and he was Jean-Luc, the years between them meant nothing.

'Oh, Jean-Luc.'

She was crying. She put up her hands to cover her face.

Something rustled. Jess looked down. She was wearing an apple-green skirt with sprays of gold embroidery, looped back over a hooped petticoat of dull gold. Creamy lace frothed at the low neckline of the bodice. She could feel the tight boning round her ribcage, that was making her stand straight as a dancer: if you slouched in a dress like this, you'd suffocate. A dark green velvet cloak fell from her shoulders. It was lined with yellow taffeta. She could feel the weight of the folds that dropped nearly to the ground.

She took a step backwards, her hands spread on the uncanny skirts, icy chills running through her. 'What's happening? What is it this time? This is too much! Stop it!'

No one answered. The fountain had vanished. She was standing on a velvety green lawn. In front of her there was a house. It had a brown-tiled roof and large chimneys. It was built of timber beams and lath-and-plaster, like an Elizabethan house in England. It was already old. The roof had a comfortable slight sag in the middle, and the timber and plaster had mellowed.

She went up to the house and let herself in, lifting the latch on a dark little door as if she'd been living here all her life. A passageway led her to a room with windows that overlooked the lawn. The walls and the coffered ceiling were panelled in dark, polished wood. The floor was tiled in marble squares, in a black and white geometric pattern. The windows had small leaded panes. She saw that it was summer out there. The flowerbeds were in late-summer bloom: red-hot pokers, delphiniums and Japanese anemones. Evening sunlight gilded the surface of the river that ran by at the foot of the lawn.

Jessica heard marching feet: a sound that brought visions of soldiers in uniform rank on rank. Through a doorway beyond the flowerbeds, she glimpsed a street. There was a fat, curvy old car parked by the kerb . . . *a car? how did that get there?*

A table stood in the middle of the room: dark wood

again, with a runner of green velvet down the middle. Straight-backed chairs with studded leather seats stood round it. Jean-Luc was sitting in one of the chairs.

He was dressed in blue and rose. Gold cord trimmed the pockets and the lapels of his full-skirted coat. The cuffs of his breeches were gold-laced too. His stockings were white silk, a slender sword hung at his side. His hat, which was trimmed with more gold, lay on one of the chairs. A glass pitcher filled with yellow wine stood at his elbow.

He didn't seem to know Jessica was there. He was working hard, writing or drawing something with great concentration. A sheaf of papers lay in front of him, some had spilled on to the floor. As she watched, he swept back the skirts of his coat, poured himself a glass of wine, and settled again intently to his task. She took off her cloak: bent and picked up one of the sheets of paper. All the drawings were the same but she couldn't quite make them out. When she tried to look closely, the lines dissolved.

'Jessy.' He had noticed her: but it was different. She'd never seen him look so hard, so concentrated. His grey eyes were like chips of silver in his tanned face.

'Is this how you were?' she asked him, gesturing at the rich, elaborate clothes. 'Were you an aristocrat in those days, when you lost the treasure?'

'An aristocrat?' He shrugged. 'If you like. I was rich, we were all rich and secure, in *their* eyes. But we felt poor enough, and not safe, God knows.' He gestured impatiently with the hand that held the quill pen. 'Jessy. You saw it once, entire – *la couronne*. You must describe it for me.'

'How do you mean? It was made of jewels, fitted together –'

He was trying to conceal his anxiety, but he could not.

'You must tell me! Each piece of the puzzle must be *precisely* the right shape, or it will not fit in its place.'

She wanted to help, but she was fascinated by the details of this fantasy, or dream, or whatever it was. She touched the silver gilt ringlets that lay on her shoulder. She noticed that she was wearing rings on her fingers: an emerald in brilliants, a ruby surrounded by tiny sapphires. And it was all amazingly real! She arranged her gold-sprigged skirts:

'But, don't you know?'

'I knew.' He struggled to keep his voice calm. 'But I have forgotten. *I have lost it.*'

'I could try to draw it,' she offered. She thought she could. It was true, as she had told him once: she remembered every detail. 'I'm good at *imaging things* in my mind, everyone says so. It's a knack. I do good diagrams. If you had a computer with graphics software, that would be even better –'

But the marching feet were coming nearer: *slam, slam, slam.* She knew that the clothes they were wearing were from the eighteenth century, the time of the French Revolution. Was that the mob of peasants coming to storm the castle of Rochers?

Jean-Luc had leapt up and was fingering a panelled wall, his ear against the wood. He muttered: 'Ha, got it,' and a sheet of wood slid away, revealing dark space. 'Up here, quickly.'

There was a staircase in the thickness of the wall. It was very narrow. Jessica bundled her gold and green skirts in front of her. They climbed until she was breathless. 'You know all the secret passages,' she gasped. 'But that time, when you left me and Paddy in the *oubliette*, the caretaker who got us out said there wasn't one –'

'What night?' He opened another secret door, into a

shadowy room: he looked back. 'Rochers has many secrets. They don't know everything.'

Something moved. A shadowy figure fell on Jean-Luc. Jess's hand groped instinctively for a weapon. She found a knife hidden in the boned bodice of her dress. But by the time she'd pulled it out the fight was over.

'Quickly . . .' Jean-Luc grabbed her arm. He looked back at the fallen body. 'That was my dream,' he whispered. 'To fight in darkness, a young hero. It didn't happen. *Quickly, now* . . .'

They crept on again, past rooms in which men were talking earnestly and sometimes angrily. Sometimes there were guards posted at the doors, and Jean-Luc pulled her back into shadow and found another way. They reached the top of a flight of stairs, Jean-Luc wrestled with a hatch-cover overhead.

'Up!'

He lifted her, she grabbed a dusty sill and pulled herself through. Jean-Luc followed. They were in a narrow crawl-space between two floors: lath-and-plaster above and below them.

'Be very careful,' Jean-Luc warned her, tenderly. 'Put your weight on the joists, not on the ceiling. You will have to wriggle, you see, like a little caterpillar.'

She wondered why he was suddenly talking to her as if she was a child. He wormed in beside her, his head between his shoulders and knees up by his ears. It would have been funny if he hadn't looked so desperate, and if he wasn't smiling in that weird, strained way, as if he was reassuring a child in a situation where he knew there was nothing reassuring . . .

'A little more,' he coaxed. 'And you will be safe. Don't be afraid, we will look after you. All's well.'

Jess was bewildered. 'But what about the treasure?'

'Won't you try to be a little caterpillar? Please?'

They wriggled and crawled. There were people moving below. Jessica nearly slipped at one point, and lay with her cheek against a length of rough wood, her heart thumping. She didn't know what fate awaited them if they were caught, but Jean-Luc's terror was infectious. Her mouth was dry and she was shaking with dread.

They came out of the crawl-space into a loft that smelled of hay. A woman was there, alone: crouched intently, with something like headphones over her ears. She hid her equipment, quickly and calmly, as Jean-Luc and Jess tumbled in on her. When she saw Jean-Luc, she spoke to him and led them down through the quiet house. It was night, and everyone else was asleep. *'Doucement,'* she said, *softly!* Then she said, *'Bonne chance, p'tite,'* – good luck, little one – and kissed Jess.

But her face, in the light of the single candle that lit that closely shuttered house, was pale and cold. The eyes were sunken in bruised pits. She lifted her hand to wave goodbye. Her arm moved strangely, as if it was jointed in extra places.

*She's dead!* thought Jess.

They were out of doors. Jean-Luc gripped her hand and tugged her along. 'Quickly,' he gasped. There were lights in the dark that shouldn't be there. Jean-Luc's voice was full of panic. Jess felt a wail of terror and misery rising in her throat, but though she was only a little girl she knew that she *must never cry out.* He had drawn his sword, faint light gleamed on the metal. But it had changed. It was blue-black, with a long glistening barrel, machined chambers, a grip that looked overlarge in Jean-Luc's young hand. What was a modern pistol doing in an eighteenth century fantasy?

Then everything shifted. They were in a small bare room. Light fell from a naked bulb, there was a spy-hatch in the grey metal door. Jean-Luc turned to her. His youth had vanished. He looked old and weary.

'The twentieth of August,' he muttered. 'No. I have nothing to tell you. Nothing . . .'

'We've been here before,' she said.

It was the room of the first vision she'd shared with him: the cold cell, whose air breathed terror and misery and hopeless regrets. She knew that something had been left out, something vital. But it was Jean-Luc's experience, not hers. She couldn't make him go back, and show her what had happened to bring him to this terrible end. She could only feel the missing pieces, some part of the story he could not bear to face . . .

'What about the treasure?'

'The treasure?' he repeated. 'But you have it, Jessy. I lost it, and you found it. Isn't that so?'

'But it's gone!' she wailed, remembering what had happened in the real world. 'They took it back! It's not fair! Why won't they leave you alone!'

'They want my life,' he said. 'I have tried to give it to them, but it's no use. They are not satisfied.'

'*Have you got it?*' whispered a small voice in the shadows.

Other voices took up the question. They were young, but they were endlessly cruel. They gathered, eyes and teeth glinting. Jess felt the force of a judgement without mercy, a pitiless hunger. The terrible children were closing in.

'Please!' cried Jean-Luc. 'Jessy, *please* –'


And then she was standing in the porch of the chapel in the French garden. It was dark in there and she was frightened. She walked quickly down the gravel path. At every step she felt the urge to look back. *They were following her.*

On the streets of London it was Christmas time. Lights sparkled. Shop windows were jolly with evergreen boughs and baubles and scarlet ribbons. Jessica walked with her head down to the tube station. *Don't look back*.

She'd just missed a train. The platform was eerily empty for several minutes; a strange lull in the rush-hour bedlam. When it came, her train was empty too. There must have been a snarl-up. On some other station, packed hordes of people waited in helpless misery . . . Jessica was afraid to sit alone. She stumbled down the brightly-lit carriage to where three black men were sitting together: squeezed past the one who was sitting on his own and huddled against the window. They were big men, dressed well but aggressively. They had razored hair and black leather jackets, one of them twisted a huge gold ring on his little finger. But there was something quiet about them: something comforting and sane. The one with the ring glanced up as Jess edged by, with a half smile. *They'll protect me*, she thought.

But as the train rattled along she realized that no one was going to protect her. The three men were grown-up strangers with their own lives, their own troubles. After a couple of stops they got off together and Jess was left alone: afraid of every movement, seeing the nasty children everywhere out of the corner of her eye. She thought that she must look the way Jean-Luc looked when she met him in the garden. Like a hunted thing.

'*I haven't got it*,' she whispered. 'I haven't!'

They were not satisfied. They would never be satisfied. Oh, Jean-Luc. What can I do?

# Five

J ESS MADE DRAWINGS OF *LA COURONNE*, THE LOST
treasure as she had seen it in her vision in the castle
chapel. She didn't know what Jean-Luc's powers were. If
he could travel in time, if he could conjure up different
worlds and lead her into them, then why couldn't he
recreate something: if he had an exact image?

The children didn't have the jewelled crown, because
if they had it surely Jean-Luc would be free. He had lost
it, and then Jess had lost it. But it could be replaced . . .
remade. Otherwise, why had he kept asking her to
describe the crown? Why did he keep trying to draw it
himself? She didn't know if her idea made sense. But she
had to try something. She had to *suspend disbelief* – the
way the English teacher at school said you should, to
believe in *Romeo and Juliet*. She had to suspend disbelief
and try anything crazy, that might help him.

She drew it in pencil, in felt tips, in pen and ink. She
wasn't satisfied with any of these versions. She asked
Adam if she could borrow his computer, and worked for
ages with his paintbox programme. She came up with a

*couronne* that was an improvement, anyway. There was no way she could put in the detail her mind's eye demanded, she'd need much better software for that. But she was as near as she was going to get.

At home they had a black and white dot matrix printer, which was crotchety and old and useless. She asked Adam if he could get a colour laser print done at college. He said he'd see: but being Adam he was better than his word. He gave her back the disc a day later, with five beautiful prints of the jewelled crown.

'This is pretty,' he said. 'Sorry I forgot to hand it over last night. What is it? A portrait of the latest new molecule you've invented, you child prodigy?' He turned the paper slowly around in his clumsy hands.

'It isn't a *molecule*,' she snapped. She whisked the prints away from him. 'It's none of your business.'

The social services had arranged for Adam to have a taxi to take him to college some mornings, to spare Mum and Dad the juggling between that long drive and their working hours. The driver was waiting in the street: his horn tooted. But Adam had spotted the disappointment and misery Jess tried to hide.

'It turned out wrong. Was it so important? Can I help?'

At that moment Jess hated Adam, because he had implied that Jean-Luc was a daydream. Her frustration boiled up.

'No you can't,' she snarled. 'Can't anything happen in this house, that isn't to do with you?'

'Look,' said Adam, 'I was meaning to ask you . . . Did you try what I said, about a different route?'

She stared at him. It was over a week since she'd come to his room in the middle of the night, and tried to tell him her story. She had not been back to the garden since last Thursday – when Jean-Luc had bundled her through the secret passages, and she had been with him again in the prison cell. She had told herself she would not go back until she had something to give him.

She was nearly crying. The taxi driver tooted his horn again. 'It's none of your business,' she repeated, savagely.

'I've been thinking. What if you try asking the demon lover back here, to meet the folks?'

Adam must have forgotten that he'd practically told her straight out she was making it all up.

'I don't think that would work, somehow. Can't you leave me alone? Your limo's waiting, Mr Famous.'

'Hey, calm down,' soothed Adam. 'I can take a hint.'

He swung out to the taxi on his crutches, Mum and the driver had already stowed his chair, Mum had rushed off to get her bus. Dad was hustling Paddy, trying to get him ready for school. Jess was left with the prints. She stared at them. Adam's comment had made her flare up, because he was right. She had felt there was something wrong. The sharp colour images made it horribly obvious. This didn't look like a picture of a mediaeval jewel. It was as if her memory was a computer itself, and something had scrambled up in there. The lost treasure had been overwritten and jumbled with something else entirely.

'I don't understand,' she whispered. 'I don't understand.'

She still had nothing. She could not go back with these.

It was Thursday when Adam gave her the prints. On that Saturday, after lunch, Jess and Paddy and Mum went up into the loft to sort out the Christmas decorations. It should have been a happy occasion, one of the nice little rituals of preparing for Christmas. Jess didn't feel very cheerful, but she did her best.

Finding the Christmas decorations took no time. They

were in a neat stack of boxes that had survived a year's random attacks on Mum's orderly storage. But Mum was in a relaxed mood, and the loft had the feel of a chill, dusty haven. All three of them surrendered to the junkshop charm of it: the Raven family past. Paddy fell on a big carton of retired toys and tipped them out, and neither Mum nor Jess tried to stop him. Mum opened a chest of old clothes, saying she ought to sort some more jumble. Jess sat on the toboggan, which had been in dry dock up here since the last snowy winter, and began to leaf through holiday scrapbooks.

They made a scrapbook every year. It included pressed-flowers, postcards, maps of towns, admission tickets and restaurant bills – with the best of their photos stuck in at relevant points, and little drawings animating the margins. There was no sense in it really. The books were soon shifted up to the loft to gather dust, and rarely looked at again. But the making was fun. It was much more satisfying than slotting naked photographs into plastic sleeves in an ordinary album.

Traditionally Mum was in charge of the creation of this family art, but Jess was planning to take over. She flipped the pages of the latest in the series: the summer of Rochers-Jumeaux. Just for a moment, she was not thinking of the desperate problem of Jean-Luc . . . At six, Paddy had reached the age where he didn't think it was worth taking a photo unless someone had a banana in their ear. It was a pity, he used to look so sweet. In this lot there was hardly a picture that wasn't marred by having Comic Little Boy in the middle of it. Then there were Paddy's own dire efforts: headless Ravens, blobby apparitions of six-year-old thumb. But the point of the scrapbook was memory, not skill.

There were no pictures of Rochers. It must have been Mum who'd made that decision. But Jess couldn't remember, come to think of it, anyone taking any photos.

'*Vrrrm, vrrm,*' muttered Paddy contentedly. '*Chuff, chuff, chuff.*' He'd found the cheap toy train (now battery-less and battered) that he used to love when he was three.

'You don't remember this,' sighed Mum, holding up a long white embroidered skirt. 'It was years before your time. Even before Adam's time. Hardly worn, too. D'you think it's pretty? I wonder if I could get into it. Probably not.'

'You're not fat!'

'Ah, no. But the waist goes. If you have three children, the waist goes. Unless you're some kind of superwoman.'

She held the pretty, faded skirt against her, and spread the embroidered folds. 'How time flies,' she murmured. 'How much harder life turns out, than you imagine it when you are young . . .'

Jess knew she was thinking of Adam. Suddenly her own eyes blurred with tears. The loft was cold. It was piled with dead hopes, lost years, stolen lives.

'It never suited me,' said Mum. 'And it's gone all yellow in the creases.' She tossed the skirt aside.

Jess ducked her head over the scrapbook, surreptitiously wiping her eyes. She turned a page, and found the English Language tourist leaflet from Rochers, tucked in with the pictures from the last campsite. She remembered the swallows in the orchard, the dragonflies that Adam had called *melusines* playing over the stream . . . There was a picture from their last walk. That place with the picnic tables: with Jess asleep, her mouth dopily open. Oh, great. Of course no brother could resist that one.

The Rochers leaflet was in her hand. She started to read it, without thinking. There was more about the

Virgin of the Chaplet than she had read when she was in the chapel: it went on over the page . . . '*Sadly the Black Virgin's great treasure, the Christ Child's jewelled crown – thought to represent the crown of thorns – was destroyed. After the Terror, the stones were traced to a Paris jeweller, who had recut and reset them to disguise their identity. The gold had been melted down. Three remarkable emeralds were recovered, and can be seen in the cathedral treasury at . . .*'

Jess stared at the words: stunned.

'*La couronne*. It doesn't exist!'

In the picture of Jess asleep, a group of figures stood beside the bench. But there'd been no one else at the viewpoint, except Jess and Adam and Paddy. She peered closer, cold tremors running through her. Surely those ragged creatures hadn't been there a moment ago. *They shouldn't be there* . . .

'What doesn't exist? What are you looking at, Jess?'

'Nothing.' She shut the scrapbook. 'Can we go down? It's freezing up here.'

She wanted the Rochers leaflet. But she didn't dare to open the scrapbook again. She had drawn the children out of hiding, and Mum's sadness had given them something to feed on. She could feel them, the lost souls. They were thickening in the dusty air. In a moment they'd be visible, and Jess thought she'd go mad.

'Let's get *down*,' she cried. 'Come on!'

'*Chuff, Vrrrm* . . .' Paddy hadn't played trains in years, he kept forgetting to make the right noise. '*Vrrrm* . . .'

'Get out of the camping gear, Paddy.' said Mum sharply.

Too late. The tottering pile made by Jess when she was searching up here weeks ago, fell apart in a messy avalanche.

'Oh *Jess*. Couldn't you watch him?'

Jess could have screamed. The camping things had spewed over the edge of the boarding, beyond the reach of the light, into black shadow under the slope of the roof. Paddy was crawling after them. She grabbed him by the shoulders, gripping him so hard she made him yelp. 'I didn't do it on purpose!' he wailed.

'Get *out*! Leave it!' She dragged her little brother into the light, and thumped him down on the toboggan. Paddy began to sob.

'Jess!' exclaimed Mum, hurrying over. 'There's no need to be nasty to him.'

If she didn't get them away from here quickly, *they would see*. They would see the apparition that had come to Jess in the brightly-lit kitchen. She didn't think she could bear it. The tension was choking her, a cold noisome darkness was gathering round her, small filthy hands were reaching out from the grave.

She was on her knees in the mess of cooking pans and picnic mugs, shaking with terror . . . though nothing had happened, and there was nothing to be seen. But yes, there was. At the edge of the shadow, between a ceiling-joist and the wadded fibreglass insulation, lay something like a trickle of dried blood. She reached out and pulled. 'Be careful,' piped Paddy smugly, from the safety of Mum's arms. 'You'll go through the ceiling!'

Jess held the brocade drawstring bag in her hands.

'Brrr, it *is* cold,' complained Mum. 'Leave that stuff, Jess. We can tidy up another time. Let's get the boxes down.'

She left them sorting baubles and escaped to her room. She laid the treasure bag on her desk, beside the colour prints of her failed attempt to draw the lost treasure.

It must have been there all along.

It was exactly as she remembered it: a soft bag of thick material. The brocade was darkened with age but colour gleamed in the folds. She could feel the same hard shape inside. It didn't rattle. Something small . . . She imagined the jewels wrapped in cotton wool or something: the filigree wreath of colour that she had tried to conjure on to the computer screen. Priceless emeralds and rubies don't have to be great chunks of things.

'*But it doesn't exist*,' she whispered, aloud: mystified.

The Rochers leaflet said the crown had been destroyed two hundred years ago . . . Well, the leaflet had it wrong. *This was the treasure.* It had to be. She remembered that she was dealing with a world that had different rules, or no rules at all. The children had made her see them in that photograph, maybe they'd made her read something that wasn't there, to trick her.

Look inside. She must look inside.

She stared at the bag. It breathed darkness, and a dank prison-smell. Her bedroom began to be filled, as the loft had been filled, with the children's terrible presence, their hunger . . .

Jess whimpered. She grabbed the bag, and stuffed it in her pocket. She grabbed the prints too, and ran from the room.

She slipped out to the phone booth on the next street, and called Noelle. The terror had left her, she felt like an idiot.

'Noelle, I want you to do something for me.'

'What?'

'I'm in a phone box. I'll be at home in a few minutes. I want you to phone me there, and ask me to see a film with you.'

There was a surprised silence. Noelle and Jessica were inseparable friends at school. But they lived too far apart, in London terms, for casual comings and goings at other times. And it was Christmas: and they both had demanding family commitments.

'Oh. Is it something very special you want to see?'

Jess drew a breath. Better come straight out with it. Noelle hated people weaseling around when they wanted something.

'I don't want to see anything. I want to meet someone and I want you to cover for me.'

Another silence.

'Jess. How could you do this to me? I HATE telling lies.'

'Please, Noe. It's desperately, desperately important.'

'Is it a boy?'

'Yes . . . In a way, yes.'

Noelle muttered bitterly, fell ominously silent again for a while: and finally agreed. 'Well, all right. But you'd better not be getting in any trouble.'

Jess could not promise that.

'I'll pay you back,' she vowed.

'Don't talk that way. We're mates. Just don't land me in bother. You know what my mum thinks about lying.'

They agreed a story and arranged the details. Jess went home and found Dad and Adam back from their shopping expedition. Everybody was having cups of tea and mince pies. The phone duly rang. Jess arranged to meet Noelle, and go to an early show at a cinema in the centre of London.

'Has anyone seen my *A to Z*? It's okay, got it.'

'This is unexpected,' complained Dad. Saturday teatimes were sacred. Because of Adam, every hour the Ravens spent together as a family verged on being *sacred*. You weren't supposed to want to go off on your own. It could get wearing.

'I won't be late, Dad. I'd just like to see something, for once, *before* it comes out on video.'

'Leave her alone,' Mum broke in. 'Let her do something on the spur of the moment. For heaven's sake, she'll be with Noelle and it's practically the middle of the afternoon.'

'I'll give you a lift,' decided Dad, unwilling to let go.

'No! I've *told* you, Dad. You shouldn't *use* the car when you don't have to. Don't you care about this planet?'

'The Private Car is an Abomination!' intoned Adam, folding his hands and raising his eyes piously.

'A-a-a-men!' Mum responded.

She left them laughing.


It was afternoon, but it was the second week of December. It was already cold dusk when she reached that dead-alive patch of streets. The first time she met Jean-Luc here she had been lost. She remembered sitting with him on the bench by the fountain, the street guide open between them. He had shown her the way. He'd been a grown-up foreigner who knew this obscure part of London quite well, as if he'd visited often. She had thought it odd, because the Jean-Luc she'd met before hadn't seemed old enough.

If she'd known how much stranger things were going to get!

The streets were as empty as they had been that day. Rubbish drifted on the empty pavements. Winter skeletons of buddleia and willowherb rose in odd gaps between buildings. It looked the same as on a weekday, but it felt different. She was afraid – as she approached the unnamed scrap of green marked in her *A to Z* – that the French garden would have disappeared. She would reach the spot and find dusty office fronts continuing unbroken. Or she would find a park she didn't recognize: no gravel paths, no fountains, no chapel. Everybody dreams of finding the way into a magic garden, and sometimes the dream comes true. But if you try hard, if you ask too much, then suddenly you find that the door is shut. The secret garden is gone and you have nothing left to prove it was ever there.

*Bring him home to meet the folks*! She remembered Adam's suggestion, bitterly. She did not know if he was a ghost or *what* he was, but she knew she was never going to be able to bring Jean-Luc home. She would never be able to trace him by normal means in the real world, the garden was their only link. She hurried past the window of a dingy wholesale clothes suppliers. A bright orange minishift flashed in the middle of the display. Who would ever want to wear that? Her fist, in her pocket, closed over the brocade bag. It was still solid, at least. It hadn't disappeared.

She walked on. She was shivering, but not from the cold. She reached the street where red wooden gates on a corner opened on to a cobbled stable-yard. In the *A to Z* it was called Brewery St. The unromantic name steadied her. Brewery Street must be real! In the dusty doorways, the plates of dead businesses were still ranked like memorial tablets. And there were the gates.

She rushed across the road. A shock went through her as if she'd touched an electric cable: they were locked. There was a massive chain holding them together, fastened with a padlock the size of Jessica's fist. She grasped the wrought iron and stared through. The flowerbeds looked drab. She could see the chapel, and the leafless trees beyond.

'Jean-Luc!'

She tugged at the padlocked chain.

'Jean-Luc! I'm here! I came back!'

A figure came towards her. Jessica's heart stood still. But it was an old man in faded blue overalls, dragging a stiff-bristled broom. He peered at her with a surly expression.

'Clear off.'

'I just want to –'

'Can't you read?' He jabbed a gnarled finger at a board that Jess had never noticed before. She couldn't read the gilt lettering, in this poor light.

'Saturdays, the memorial garden is closed at four.'

'But it isn't. It's barely half past three!'

'I said *clear off*. Are you deaf?'

Jess took a good look at the gates. She walked away.

She wandered until she found a poky sandwich bar that was actually open, went in and ordered a sandwich and a cup of hot chocolate. It was a pity this wasn't France. In France you could sit with one cup of chocolate for a week, and nobody in the café would give you aggravation. She would bet that in this place, the fat woman behind the counter would start wiping Jess's table in a pointed way after ten minutes, and throw her out bodily in half an hour . . . What can a young girl do, if she needs to hang about on the streets of London, and avoid attention?

She could always sit in a doorway, and stick her hat on the pavement in front of her. She'd be invisible then. No one would think *that* was strange.

She'd thought of asking the gardener: *what time do you get off?* But that would have been a little too cheeky. Wait until dark. He couldn't work in the dark. He'd be gone by five. She was prepared, it didn't matter. She hadn't made any plan, when she ran out and phoned Noelle. But she'd known she needed time: and the way things were at home, that meant she needed an alibi. This was going to be different from the other meetings. She was going to ask the questions that had to be asked. She was going to do whatever had to be done, no more running and hiding. She had the treasure. She would face the children, she would hand over Jean-Luc's ransom. But *not until she was sure they would set him free.*

Jess shuddered. How could she possibly bargain with them . . . the unquiet dead? She picked up her cheese sandwich and started to eat it, mechanically. One thing at a time. She had to get into the garden, and Jean-Luc had to be there. Then, what? She didn't know. She would find out.

At five o'clock, Brewery Street was badly lit and deserted. With a black jockey-cap pulled down over her hair, black jacket and leggings, Jess was invisible. She slipped out her torch and ran the beam over the red brick pillars that supported the gates. Noe would soon tell you, Jess thought, that those pillars were in a French style. Noelle loved poring over books full of photographs of buildings. Why were they here? She had never wondered before. She'd half thought the garden *was* magic. It was a piece of France magically here for her and Jean-Luc. It didn't need a real-world explanation. She shone her torch over the lettered board.

This gar en is dedicated by the people of Lo don, to the m n and women, French and of Fre ch origin, who fought and died in the secret service of the S.O.E., French section, and of the Resistance. 1940–1945

It looked as if the same thing was written in French, underneath.

She climbed the gate. It was easy, there were plenty of footholds in the ironwork. She didn't need her torch. The unlight of city darkness was enough for her to find her way. The porch of the chapel was open. The inner doors were locked. Two benches faced each other, against the walls. She sat down, one hand closed over the brocade bag, the other holding the sheets of printer paper inside her jacket.

She was alone.

Adam was right. She had always been alone in the garden. She had stepped in here one day, and had imagined Jean-Luc, the boy she met in France, because she *needed someone*. She had come back all those times, through October, November, December, and walked the dull paths, sat and stared at the fountain: and imagined that she had a dream companion, a quest, a perilous adventure. She'd got in the habit of slipping in here for a few minutes on her way home from school, the rest was fantasy. That was the truth.

She sat on the bench for what seemed a long time.

'Jessy?'

No one else said her name quite like that.

He was not in the porch. She stood up and tried the inner doors. This time they opened. The chapel was dark. She groped for a switch and found it. He was there, in a dead grey light: in his dark jacket and mudstained trousers. He was sitting in the first pew at the back.

'Hallo, Jessy.'

She looked at the memorial tablets.

'What does the inscription on the fountain mean?' she asked. 'Where it says, *From the fig tree learn its lesson*?' She knew that he would know. This was the Jean-Luc she had met the first time of all, the adult stranger who knew the French garden well.

'It's from the bible: from the New Testament. I don't know how much history of the Nazi war you learn in school. But you see, in 1940 when France was defeated, the Resistance hardly existed. Most French people believed that it was necessary to accept the Nazi victory, and make friends with Germany. For a long time, people went on as before: business as usual, as we say nowadays. But there was horror under the surface. The Jews were being rounded up and sent to the deathcamps. Innocent

French citizens, men, women and children were sent to hideous death by French police, French bureaucrats: because of a difference in religion, and imagined "difference" in what people call race. In 1944, the horror of the deathcamps was at its height. But the Resistance had grown too. At the worst hour, in the last months before the Liberation of France, it was a powerful force. So, that's what the quotation says. When the fig tree is putting out flowers and buds, then Spring is near. When resistance to evil grows strong, though hope may seem far away, still victory is near. That is the meaning, I think: a comfort for dark days.'

Jess had listened carefully. But she wasn't here to have a lesson about France in the Second World War. The *couronne* had been lost two hundred years before.

'I've brought the treasure,' she said.

'What treasure?'

'I found it in the secret passages. When we met in Rochers, at the town party. When you were with the children. Don't you remember?'

He stared at her.

'I have dreamed of that night for fifty years. This year, one night, you were there in the dream. My faithful companion. I have never known why you came to me. But I have been grateful.'

'Your *dreams*?'

'I am dreaming now.'

'But it was *real*,' she protested, 'Paddy and I, we were in the passages. We had to be pulled out of the oubliette-pit. How can real, solid things happen, in a dream?'

He shrugged. 'I don't know. Is the world of dreams unreal? Perhaps not. Past and present, time and space: perhaps these are the phantoms.'

'Jean-Luc, you're not listening! *I have the treasure.* Call them. I can free you from the terrible children.'

He smiled sadly. 'They are not terrible.'

'What? But they *are*. You told me so!'

'They are terrible to me. Because I live, and they died.'

'But they're evil, horrible.'

He shook his head at her bewilderment. 'You'd better go,' he said. 'Don't come too close. Or they will haunt you forever, as they haunt me. Sweet angel, whatever you are. Go from my mind, whatever way you came, and don't come back.'

'Jean-Luc, no. Don't give up. I'll get you out of this somehow. *They shan't have you!*'

Jean-Luc gave a sob. '*Go away*, Jessy!'

There was a thickening in the air, in the grey light between them. As she watched, it became a layering of shadow. The shadows took form: and the children were there. They gathered, taking on detail and substance. Eyes became bright and hard, limbs formed out of mist. They, the pursuers whose undying hatred held Jean-Luc in terror. They grinned at Jess, showing their rat-teeth. They were not human children, if they ever had been. They were goblins, monsters.

'Who *are* you?' she cried.

*We are the lost*.

They did not speak. Their answer shivered in her mind.

She saw the faces that she remembered from the night of the twentieth of August. *Marcel, Simone, Liliane, Jean-Claude, Jacques, Richard* . . . The walls of the chapel had gone. The children, twenty-two of them, clustered around Jean-Luc. They tugged at his coat, shoved their faces into his. *We're hungry*, they whined. *We're lonely. We want to be out in the air. Give the sun and air back to us, we cannot breathe underground*.

Something changed. They stopped pestering him and moved away: they stood together in a huddle, watching him. The battered hand-me-down clothes fell from their scrawny limbs. Marcel began to scream hoarsely: a horrible sound, like a buzz-saw, going on and on. His skin burst out welts and vile sores. Another boy started to pull out his own teeth one by one, grinning bloodily between tugs. Another took one hand in the other and pulled until he'd pulled his shoulder out of joint. One of the small girls – it was Rachel, who had stolen Jess's waist pouch – rose into the air, feet dangling. She dropped her head sideways and stuck out her tongue.

'Stop it!' yelled Jess. 'You disgusting little *brutes*, STOP IT. You can't frighten me with a bunch of Hallowe'en tricks!'

But the sound of her words vanished. She watched, powerless, as one child after another played out an ugly scene and vanished. The group that remained stood quietly. They were dressed in other rags now, all of them the same. They shuffled in a line, their faces bowed. Some of them were crying softly, Jean-Luc stood up and took his place among them. He was like someone hypnotized and unable to defend himself.

'*Where are you going?*'

No answer. The children and their guardian passed one by one through a door she could not see, and disappeared.

'Jean-Luc, don't go with them . . . Stay with me!'

He looked back, over his shoulder.

'*Remember the names. It's important to remember the names.*'

'*Jean-Luc!*'

He was gone. The children had stolen him, they had carried him away into their hideous goblin world.

Her own reality gathered itself again around her. She was in the porch of the chapel in the French garden. She was breathing as if she'd been running, and her face was wet with tears. It was like waking from someone else's nightmare. She came fully awake: started violently, and grabbed at both her treasures. The paper crackled. The brocade bag was still solid in her hand.

'The children didn't take them,' she whimpered. 'Why not? It's not fair. They took Jean-Luc instead.'

She had brought the bag, and her drawings of *la couronne*. She'd done and dared everything that seemed asked of her, and she had not saved him. She had not broken the evil spell. 'But he said he was *alive*.' She heard the sound of her own voice, shaky and puzzled. 'If he's alive, how can he be with the ghosts?'

It was very dark in the porch, almost as dark as it had been in the secret passages under the château. She switched on her torch, picked up the brocade bag, and loosened the drawstring.

The hard-edged object was not a mediaeval casket, or anything from the eighteenth century. It was a battered French tobacco tin. It looked old, but not very old. She opened the lid, and shone her torch inside.

She saw the children.

She stared for a moment, more bewildered than ever. She lifted the yellowed cutting out and studied a column of small, blurred photos. She didn't recognize any of the faces – except Marcel: who could forget that little monster! But she was sure that these were some of the nasty children. The newsprint was blurred and faded from being folded and refolded. She could not read a word of it, but she could read the date. It was only a year or two old. There was another piece of paper underneath, it was thicker than the other and had once been white. It carried a list of names, in angular copperplate handwriting. The ink had faded to the colour of dried blood, but it could still be read. Beside some of the names there were comments in French, some in very faded pencil. It looked a little like a school report. Jess couldn't understand all of it: but she made out some of the meaning.

> Marcel Muller   10   *both parents certainly dead;*
> Simone Benguigui   12   *some family in America?;*
> Liliane ?   8?   *she doesn't remember anything;*
> Jean-Claude Halpern   8   *this one won't talk;*
> Jacques Kohn   7   *don't try to take the thing made of*
> *rag from him.*
> Richard Mayer   11   *does not sleep . . . bad cough.*
> Lea Klein-Leiber   9?   *sore on r.hand will not heal,*
> *should see a doctor if possible?*

There was nothing else in the bag, except a squashed grey, shapeless rag that had once been a child's sock. It had two dark knots (meant to be eyes?) sewn into the toe. She put the papers back in the tin, and replaced the lid carefully: these things were precious. This was the treasure that Jean-Luc had lost, to his great grief.

'I still don't understand!' she whispered. 'What happened? What really happened?'

The porch vanished. She was standing out of doors. The air was warm. There was grass under her feet. She looked up, craned her head back and saw what she expected to see: the floodlit *donjon* tower, cut out against a deep blue sky. There were soft sounds coming towards her.

It was Jean-Luc, with his little flock of bad children. The children were being kept in hiding in the secret passages under the ruined part of the château, under the very noses of their enemies, who ruled the region from the Tour de Garde. From here they would be taken by skilled guides over the mountains to Switzerland. Jess knew all this, without knowing how she knew. Looking after this group of children wasn't easy. Many of them had been treated worse than animals in the detention camps. They had seen their parents beaten and abused, or been torn from their mothers' arms and then cared for by frightened strangers; passed from hand to hand for years. They trusted no one: they were vicious. Their guardians had to be endlessly patient.

In the middle of the night, at the dark of the moon, Jean-Luc had taken them out for some fresh air, down in the secret gorge. Now they were coming back to the western crag, to the passage in the rock under the ruined keep. There were floodlights over the Tour de Garde. The children were good at being silent. But even in the most dangerous situations they were not to be trusted. Jess heard a muffled squeal. She heard Jean-Luc mutter: '*Marcel, you little devil, leave her alone . . . Lili, stop that!*' He was exasperated: but she could hear the gentleness in his voice.

Suddenly, lights blazed out. Monster eyes glared. There were vehicles on the track that led to the ruins. They were not supposed to be there! Jess saw Jean-Luc stop dead. She heard him gasp, she *felt* the shock and horror that ran through him. She saw him trying to calm the children, whispering frantically: '*be quiet, hurry, don't be afraid, all's well . . .*'

But all was not well. There were beaters in the trees, men in uniform, moving in with confidence on their prey, Jean-Luc gave up trying to reach the entrance to the passages. He knew it would have been stopped like a fox's earth. He cried, '*Run, all of you! Run and hide . . .*' He swooped on little Rachel, the incorrigible thief: grabbed Marcel by the hand. He tried to run, with Rachel in his arms fighting like a fury, Marcel biting and clawing at the fingers that gripped his skinny wrist . . .

'*Run!*' sobbed Jess. '*Save them!*'

But Jean-Luc could not save them. And Jess could only watch, at last, the part of the nightmare that he had never shown her before. She saw what had really happened, when the nasty children and their guardian played hide-and-seek with evil, that August night fifty years ago, under the shadow of the *donjon* tower.

She saw the children rounded up, and Jean-Luc with them. She saw him at the police station, being parted forcibly from Rachel and Marcel. Marcel was sobbing *Jean-Luc, Jean-Luc.* But when the men in uniform had dragged them apart he shouted *'Traitor! Piece of filth! What did they pay you for us? Traitor . . . !'*

She saw Jean-Luc in the holding cell, sitting on the cot with the grey blanket, looking at the spy-hatch in the metal door. She knew what he was seeing as he stared into space. Those eyes, those reaching hands. Jean-Luc was not guilty, but she understood why guilt and shame would haunt him. The childrens' guardian had not betrayed them. But they would die believing that he had.


And then she was back again, in the porch of the chapel. She felt the dull chill of a December night settle around her, as she woke from someone else's nightmare.

'Jean-Luc?'

He was gone. She was alone.

She buried her face in her hands.

*'Why me? Why me?'*

No one answered. She put the tobacco tin back in the brocade bag. She folded her pictures of the crown, her useless efforts. Her idea about *la couronne* had been a complete mistake, apparently. She shoved them and the bag into her pocket, and looked at her watch. It was six o'clock in London, and two weeks before Christmas.

She climbed over the gate. The street was still deserted. She walked quickly, looking back often over her shoulder. A little cold wind had started up. It rustled like the pattering of small feet. When she reached a brightly-lit street with traffic on it; and people, she turned and shouted. *'Leave me alone!'*

A couple stopped: a man and a woman in warm, bright, winter clothes. 'Is someone giving you trouble?' asked the man.

'No,' said Jess. 'Thank you.'

She was waiting outside the cinema when Noelle emerged.

The bright lights shone on Noelle's dark face as she came out of the crowd. Jess stared. *Suppose they came for you*, she thought. *Suppose they came for you, because you're different: to take you away to the camps, like those children.* What would I do?

*What would I do?*

'Well,' said her friend, coming up and looking her over. 'You look as if you've been having a mega-wonderful time, I don't think.'

'Was the movie all right?'

'It wasn't bad.' Noelle was not in a good temper. 'If you like going to the cinema alone. Which I don't.'

'I'm really sorry, and I really owe you –' Jess started, and looked sharply into the crowd of cinema-goers.

'What's up? Someone bite you?'

'No . . . I thought I heard someone speaking French.'

Noelle looked puzzled. 'Well, why not? This is the centre of London. It's crawling with foreigners, all year round.'

'I suppose so,' muttered Jess. 'Sorry.'

Noelle sighed. 'Want some chips?'

'No. I'd better be getting back.' Noelle deserved an explanation, but she was the last person on earth to believe in ghosts. 'Look, I'll tell you about it. I promise. But . . . not now.'

'Okay. You look rotten, I must say. G'night. Safe home.'

She could feel Noelle's eyes on her back until she reached a corner and the cinema passed out of sight. The lighted entrance of her station beckoned. *Was it a good film?* She rehearsed her parents' innocent questions. *Yeah, I suppose so. A bit too scary* . . . Maybe it was a love story they were supposed to have seen. She was supposed to have talked to Noelle and found out what the film was like, but she'd forgotten to do that. She couldn't even remember the title. She'd manage somehow. It didn't seem important.

The tiled walls in the bleak underground light made her think of prisons. A train whooshed away as she reached the last flight of stairs. A sheet of crumpled newspaper flapped along the platform. It looked like a child with skinny arms wrapped around its head to ward off blows . . . She winced and closed her eyes.

She had been chosen as a witness, and now she knew the truth. If anybody asked her she could tell them: *Jean-Luc Batiste did not betray the Jewish children who were in his care, in the town of Rochers in August 1943.* But who was going to ask, after all these years? And who would ever believe Jess's story, anyhow?

'What's good is closely woven with what is bad . . .'

Jean-Luc had told her that. It didn't explain anything. But why me, she thought. *Why me?*

# Six

SHE NEEDN'T HAVE WORRIED. NO ONE ASKED HER about the film. When Jess came in from the street she brought a gust of cold air into an incredibly cosy scene. Mum and Dad and Paddy were making Christmas decorations. The place was littered with snippets of coloured tissue paper: scissors, glue, glitter.

'Jess! What d'you think of them?' cried Mum gaily, holding up two tissue-paper stars. 'I copied the pattern from a magazine. You stick them on the window, so the light shines through them.'

Jess had never seen her parents acting so Christmassy. Usually they behaved like most people: groaning and moaning about all the hassle, with occasional flashes of seasonal spirit to lighten things up. But she knew why they were getting involved. It was because of Adam. There would not be many more normal Christmases. By next year or the next, Adam might be completely helpless: and soon, too soon, it would be the last Christmas of all.

She swallowed hard. 'They're pretty. Where's Adam?'

'In his room,' said Dad.

'Remember to knock,' warned Mum cheerily. 'I think he's wrapping presents.'

She knocked. He called his usual imperious: 'Enter!'

He *had* been wrapping presents. 'Wait there! But you don't have to close your eyes.' He whizzed the office chair to and fro, stashing his parcels and grinning. He had a piece of tinsel garland tucked behind one ear. Jess admired the way he made that chair spin . . . He was good in his motorchair too. Sometimes she'd forget and think: he could be in the wheelchair marathon, the way he's going. But Adam would not get to be a well person in a wheelchair. Sales' Myasthenia never ended like that.

He'd have to move downstairs soon. And that would be the beginning of the end.

'I need your advice about something,' she said.

Adam cocked an eyebrow: 'Again? I thought you didn't like the last lot . . . Is it about the same problem?'

She thrust her hands in her pockets, and looked at the floor.

'Not really.'

'You aren't having trouble with the demon lover anymore?'

*'Can I just tell you, please.'*

Adam whizzed over and looked at her hard.

'But is it more ghosts and visions?'

Though he spoke lightly, she could tell he was really worried. She felt awful about the way she'd told him all that stuff in the middle of the night – as if he didn't have enough to keep him awake. But she had planned what she was going to say, this time. She wasn't going to have him worrying anymore about his sister with the nervous breakdown.

'No . . . I didn't explain very well the other night. It isn't anything like that. It's some lost property I have to return.'

She sat down on the bed.

'It's difficult. I've had these things a long time, but I didn't know I had them. I don't know how to trace the owner, but I know he wants – must want – to have them back. All I know is his name. He's called Jean-Luc Batiste, and he lives somewhere near Rochers, where we camped in August.'

Adam was nodding, looking relieved. 'The traditional thing,' he began, 'unless you want to try the police, is to advertise in a newspaper –' He stopped. His whole expression changed.

'*Jean-Luc Batiste?* Doctor Jean-Luc Batiste?'

'Doctor? His father was a doctor . . . His father was a doctor and his mother a pharmacist in a little town near Rochers, I don't know the name of the town, but there's a river . . .'

'Aulne-sur-Die,' supplied Adam.

He looked very strange, almost *angry*.

'But he's not old enough to be a doctor himself.'

'Not old?' said Adam. 'He's nearly seventy.'

He stared at her for another *long* moment, with the same suspicious, almost angry expression. He spun the chair across to his desk, hooked open a drawer and pulled out a thick manila folder. He dumped it on her knees.

'Jean-Luc Batiste. Dr Jean-Luc Batiste, the one I know, is a French scientist, or was. He's a paediatrician, a children's doctor, turned molecular biologist. He's famous, in his field. You must have heard the name from me, or from Mum and Dad. He was working on a cure for Sales' Myasthenia. He came near to modelling a synthetic version of the gene that's defective, specially adapted so it could be inserted in a virus that could be used to *infect* people like me. The virus would get itself replicated – copied, you understand about that?'

She nodded.

'And the gene would be copied along with it, the part that codes for the missing protein in my nerve-sheath cells. I'm not talking about a cure twenty years in the future. I'm talking about a working therapy, that could have saved my life. But he gave up. His team was disbanded. I don't get it, Jess. Is this some kind of joke? I do not see the point.'

Jess stared. 'I didn't know –'

'No,' snapped Adam, still angrily. 'It was three years ago. You were ten, why should you know? The research has gone off in different directions, since. No one believes anymore that what Batiste was trying can be done.'

Jess opened the folder. There were pages copied from medical journals, documents from conferences. Some of it was French and some of it was English . . . Her mind was a spinning blank.

'Jean-Luc is old. Oh, Jean-Luc is old.'

'What are you blethering about? World class scientists get old like anybody else: I mean *anybody normal*. Do you remember the day when we camped at Rochers and Mum and Dad and I went off in the Slug? We were there because it was the nearest campsite with disabled facilities, to Aulne-sur-Die. We kept it quiet. We knew we were being fools and we didn't want you kids involved. We went to Aulne-sur-Die, and asked to see the great man. I don't know what we thought we were going to achieve. I've rarely felt such an idiot in my life. His housekeeper turned us away at the door. Mum was very upset.'

'I remember,' whispered Jess, in a hollow voice.

'Then *what* are you trying to tell me?'

She closed the folder. It didn't help. 'I'm confused.'

'So am I!'

She realized that this was the nearest she'd come to really quarrelling with Adam since she was about six years old.

'Did something happen to him?' she pleaded. 'In the War, in the Nazi war, when he was young? Something terrible?'

Adam seemed to grow very still, in his chair.

'You really don't know?'

'I know *something*. But please tell me, Adam.'

At last his expression relaxed, as if he finally believed that Jess was not playing some kind of silly game.

'In 1943,' he said, 'the town of Rochers was a station on what they call an underground railway. In August of that year a group of Jewish children was passing through, on the way to a mountain escape route over into Switzerland. But things went wrong. The guides were getting scared. The children had to stay in Rochers for longer than anyone had planned. They were hiding in the secret passages under the ruined part of the castle. Jean-Luc Batiste was seventeen. He was one of the young people assigned to look after the children. Well, one night the Nazis came and rounded up the lot. Someone had betrayed them.'

'It wasn't Jean-Luc!'

Her brother gave her a curious look.

'Jean-Luc was arrested with them,' he went on. 'He was sent off to forced labour in Germany. The children all died. He survived, and became a doctor specializing in children's diseases. Later he went into pure research and nearly discovered a cure for my problem. But then, three years ago, a scandal broke. Someone wrote a book about collaborators in the Second World War: people who'd helped the Nazis or been Nazis themselves, and got away with it. One of the revelations was that Dr Jean-Luc Batiste, when he was seventeen, had betrayed those children. He'd been responsible for sending twenty-two children, who were in his care and trusted him, to the deathcamps.

'*It isn't true!*'

'No one thought it was,' said Adam. 'The writer of the book later admitted he was lying about that one. Some of his stories were true, but some were pure scandal-journalism. He ended up in court, over another of his denouncements. But Dr Batiste behaved strangely for an innocent man. He didn't sue. He gave up his work, refused to defend himself, and went back to Aulne-sur-Die: where he lives more or less in hiding, hardly leaving the house.

'That's the whole story, Jess.' Adam looked stern. 'Now you tell me, what's it got to do with you?'

Jess pulled the brocade bag from her pocket. She took out the tobacco tin, opened it and handed it to him.

'I . . . I found this, when we were in Rochers. I stuck it in my rucksack and forgot about it. When I remembered it again, it had gone. I thought I'd lost it. But it turned up, today when we were getting down the Christmas decorations. I think he wants it back.'

Adam took out the yellowed cuttings, and the rag-thing, and the list of names. He turned them over on his knees. Jess noticed how gentle his clumsy hands could be: and how thin he was getting. Mum and Dad did *hours* of physio with him every day. But it wasn't enough. Nothing would be enough, short of a miracle.

Adam looked at the papers in silence. In the bathroom, next-door, bathwater was running. They could hear Paddy's cheerful voice, and Mum's quieter answers.

'I think you're right,' said Adam softly, reading. 'He should have these things. It seems like they traced what had happened to some of the children . . . poor devils. Poor Dr Batiste.'

'What should we do?'

'Send them to him, obviously.' Adam hesitated. 'I'd hate them to get lost in the post. We could phone him up, I have a number.'

Jess felt the blood drain from her face.

'No!' She couldn't imagine that conversation.

He nodded. 'You're right. I wouldn't want a stranger ringing me up about this. I don't think we'd get past the housekeeper, anyway. We can make copies, and send them to him with a letter.'

Jess swallowed hard. 'You write. But tell him, it's Jess Raven who found the treasure.'

Adam looked a little surprised. 'Sure. I won't steal your thunder.' He sighed. His hands fumbled as he closed the tobacco-tin lid over the fragile relics. 'What a coincidence. I need desperately to talk to the grand old man of Sales' Disease research, and you pick up his wartime souvenirs.'

'Yes,' she agreed. 'Isn't it strange.'

To her own surprise, Jess burst into desolate tears.


Christmas got in the way, as it tends to get in the way of most things. Adam wrote to Dr Batiste in the New Year. Jess had a birthday, life went on. For weeks they heard nothing. They were glad they hadn't told their parents. Mum and Dad would have been bound to get excited about this chance to make personal contact with the great man: and they'd have been disappointed all over again. Adam and Jess didn't talk to each other about their own disappointment.

Jess was puzzled. But she wasn't surprised. Jean-Luc had vanished from her life as she'd always known he would, with no explanations. She didn't go back to the French garden. She knew he would not meet her there again.

But at the end of February, a letter came. It was addressed to Jess and Adam's parents. It invited them, and Adam and Jess, to Aulne-sur-Die. Dr Batiste was very, very grateful that his lost property had been found. He wanted Jess to hand it over in person, and he wanted to meet Adam, whose name he remembered. He was sorry he had not been able to see the Ravens in August.

You don't question a summons like that. It took another couple of weeks to arrange everything: to book a flight and a hire car at the other end, to arrange for Paddy to spend a week with Dad's sister's family . . . things like that. Jess's school and the college made no problem about Adam and Jess having time off.

It was a mild day in March, when they came to Aulne-sur-Die. The river Die ran beside the main road, across a field. Jess watched it through the window of the hired Renault. The willows hung over the brown water still, as they had done fifty-odd years ago. No one had spoken much on the drive. As Aulne drew near nobody said a word. They crossed a bridge. The river vanished behind the houses. It was strange to see a French town in early spring. It was a sleepy place, picturesque in a quiet way.

Mum was driving. She found her way to Dr Batiste's house without any problem. They got out of the car. Adam wasn't using the chair. He walked with his stick, remarkably firmly. Jess stared at the old timbered house, the mellow plaster between the beams: the brown-tiled roof. It was right on the street. But there was a side entrance, under an archway. She glimpsed the passage to the garden.

'What's the matter, Jess?'

'Nothing.'

The housekeeper showed Mum and Dad and Adam upstairs to Dr Batiste's study. Jess was asked to stay below.

She waited in a room that was panelled in dark wood. She looked through the small-paned windows at the garden, where the river ran at the foot of the lawn. 'Delphiniums,' she whispered. 'Red-hot pokers.' There were crocuses and early daffodils flowering in the long beds.

'It's an English garden,' said Dr Batiste's house-keeper. 'Madame, Monsieur the doctor's mother made it. She loved gardening: Monsieur also. It's a great comfort to him.'

Jess touched the backs of the chairs with the studded leather seats. There was no velvet runner on the table. A bowl full of early flowering plum branches stood on a brightly-coloured mat. She looked at an engraving on the wall. She asked, in French, 'Is this the castle?'

'Yes, it is the castle from the town side, as it was a hundred years ago: and still was, when he was a boy. And I too, I was a girl. We children knew everything, everything about the ruins . . .'

Under the engraving, on a small table against the wall, stood a group of ornaments. Among them was an enamelled snuff-box. The picture on the lid showed a lady and a gentleman in eighteenth century dress, framed in a dappled wreath of branches.

'May I pick something up, madame?'

'Bien sûr, mademoiselle.'

The young lady wore a skirt of sprigged apple green over a gold petticoat. Her companion was in rose and blue, his hat under his arm. A slender blade, like a toy sword, hung at his side. Jess stared at them, feeling strange and strange indeed. She remembered what Jean-Luc had told her, the last time they met.

*You came into my dreams. I am dreaming now.*

'Poor Monsieur,' sighed the housekeeper. She was a big woman, who carried herself with dignity. There wasn't a trace of grey in her dark hair. But she must be old, if she'd been a girl when Jean-Luc was a boy. 'You know of the story, of course. How he has suffered. There are people in this very town who whisper about him. *Salopards!* As if we didn't know, all of us who lived through those times, what was done, and by whom. People say, let the old folk alone, what good can it do. But they did not leave Monsieur alone, and he is innocent. He betrayed no one!'

'I know.'

Today, the housekeeper was not the dragon who had turned Adam and Mum and Dad away. She smiled, her eyes warm. 'You understand me well, petite. It's unusual for an English.' She came over and looked critically at the ornaments, making sure Jess had put the snuff-box back exactly in place.

'It would be better for him to work again. He has energy, it is painful for him to be idle. He has taken an interest in your brother's case, which is good to see.'

A buzzer rang. The housekeeper went upstairs. Jess sat on one of the studded chairs and stared around, seeing everywhere the stuff of memory, the images that had been woven into Jean-Luc's dreams. Madame came back. 'You are to go up, mademoiselle.'

The study was an old fashioned doctor's surgery, lined with glassfronted bookcases. There was a green leather couch, and a case of antique medical instruments on a massive polished desk. Beside the windows that over-looked the garden stood a much more modern desk, with a computer workstation. A grey-haired man dressed in shabby brown tweeds was standing with his back to Jess. Adam was sitting in an armchair looking rather shaken, as if he'd had a shock that was still sinking in.

'Now you will let me write a draft for your full travel expenses,' the grey-haired man was saying as Jess came in. He spoke good English. He was writing as he spoke, evidently: for he straightened and handed a slip of paper to Jess's mum.

'Oh no,' protested Dad. He was by Adam's chair. He and Mum both looked dazed, as if they'd had the same shock as Adam. 'Can't possibly. It's too much. . .'

'Nonsense. You have no money.' said Dr Batiste briskly. 'I have money. It's nothing. I take an interest in this case. And I remain in debt.' He looked over his shoulder at Jess. His grey eyes were like chips of silver in his lined, brown face. 'Always.'

Mum, as usual the sensible one, folded the cheque and put it away.

'Thank you very much. You're right. We haven't any money.'

'And this is Jessica.'

'Yes,' said Mum, uneasily. When the letter arrived from France, Jess had told her parents the same story as she had told Adam. They felt awkward about being involved, even indirectly, in Dr Batiste's troubles. 'And she has your – your lost property.'

Dr Batiste looked gravely at the young girl.

'I should have replied sooner to your brother's letter. But it was a shock. It was hard to realize the truth.'

'I know,' she answered. 'Me, too.'

'Years ago,' he went on, 'when I used to visit London often, I discovered a memorial to the Resistance: it is a formal garden, one finds it unexpectedly, among very drab little streets. It came to mean a great deal to me. It was a refuge. I think you know it?'

—— 116 ——

'Yes.'

She gave the brocade bag to the old man who had Jean-Luc's eyes. He took it with a slight nod, and laid it aside.

'And you have something else?'

She handed him some sheets of folded paper.

He opened them and sighed, soft and long.

'Ah. *La couronne.*' He looked across to Jess's mum and dad.

'You do not know. It's a nickname I gave to the gene we were trying to model, because the complex shape of it reminded me a little of *la couronne*, the lost treasure of Rochers. If you visited the castle chapel, you will have seen the "Virgin of the Chaplet". The crown she holds, made of jewels and thorns, is a copy. The original was destroyed. My version, which I lost . . . is, in essence, here. Don't ask me to explain, some things cannot be explained: but your daughter has found it again.'

He turned to Jess. 'Jessy, we must work on this. I must show you my own images of *la couronne.*'

*Jessi* he said: her name as only Jean-Luc pronounced it. And she saw that he *was* Jean-Luc.

'Jess found it?' repeated Dad, bemused. 'Some kind of diagram as well as the other things?'

Jean-Luc ignored the question, he was studying Jess's sketches. 'Three years ago I knew. I had seen *la couronne* in my mind's eye. But it was a moment of vision, only. I had not made it concrete when the scandal broke, and the past came down like a cloud and blinded me: I was lost.'

He looked at Jess. 'Sometimes the answer to a problem comes to us in sleep, when the mind forgets its constraints. Some philosophers have thought that in our dreams, we reach a world where like minds can meet. In that country of the soul, unbearable things can be borne: unforgivable things can be forgiven . . . and visions can be shared.'

Jess remembered the circlet of living jewels, hanging in dark air. She remembered the churchy smells of incense and damp stone; and the flickering candleflames. She had guessed the truth, though she had not been sure until she saw him look at her drawings. But it was the children she thought of –

'You *didn't* betray them!' she cried.

'I did not,' pleaded Jean-Luc. 'Whoever did, let it go, I believe he died years ago . . . But I lived and *they* died, so terribly, so young. Jessy, I was innocent. But sometimes being innocent is not enough . . .'

The sunny room became unreal. They were together again in the darkness of that night. The crying children were once again being torn from Jean-Luc's arms: 'Marcel,' sobbed Jess. 'Horrible, horrible little Marcel. And Rachel, and Simone with the pigtails who sneered at me. I didn't like her. How terrible! How terrible!'

They were alone together, forgetting everything else, tears on their faces. 'Until this moment,' he whispered, 'there was no one who understood – except for an angel in my dreams. But it's important that you know, Jessy: there are no vengeful ghosts. It was in my nightmares that *they* became monsters seeking revenge.'

'I know that now,' said Jess. 'But I was being haunted by your dreams, where everything was twisted round. That's why the children seemed like horrors to me, right until the end.'

'The children are innocent, as they always were. Whatever happens after death, their sufferings are over, and they blame no one. I punished myself with phantoms, I pursued myself. But I think, at last, I will forgive myself.'

Spring sunlight fell on the heavy furniture of the old study: and on the rugs that lay on the polished boards. Outside in the English garden there was a blackbird singing. Yet for Jean-Luc and Jess the room was full of shadows, the shadows of children. They formed and slowly faded through the air, through the sun-warmed glass of the window over the garden, into the blue sky.

'*Marcel, Simone, Liliane, Jean-Claude, Jacques, Richard, Lea, Emile, René, Rachel, Henri, Victor, Marianne, Samuel, Gilbert, Claire, Jean-Marie, Ita, Jaqueline, Georges-André, Marie-Rose, Jean . . .*'

'I had lost their names,' murmured Jean-Luc. 'I could not bear to lose their names. One must forgive, but never forget. Never forget . . .'


Jessica sat at the desk, while Adam and Mum and Dad were taken downstairs again by the housekeeper. Dr Batiste looked at her sketches of *la couronne*; and at the colour prints of that strange spiky jewelled circlet, from Adam's college. He showed her his own work, the work he had abandoned three years ago. She watched complex three-dimensional images shift and turn on the computer screen, listened and answered questions. She felt like a witness at a police station, trying to assist an identikit artist. She didn't know how much help she was being. She felt young and nervous and she didn't feel that she was with *her* Jean-Luc at all. The housekeeper brought tea and cakes: which they ignored, they were too busy. It lasted about an hour.

Then it was over, and the goodbyes were said. Standing in the panelled hall, Jean-Luc shook hands with all the Ravens. Jess's turn came last. They shook hands solemnly: then suddenly they both laughed, and fell into each other's arms.

'What was all that about?' demanded Dad, as Mum started up the hire car. 'You found some papers the old man values, I know that. But you talk a lot of stuff I couldn't understand, and he sends us away, and he shows you his research, and there you are hugging each other. I can't make any sense of it.'

'Don't go on at her, Chris,' said Mum, fervently. 'Think what we've been given: hope. Don't start picking holes. Be thankful.'

Jess exchanged a glance with Adam. She knew that whatever he thought, he'd keep his curiosity to himself. She looked back through the rear window. Jean-Luc was standing in the doorway: an old man who had suffered and recovered, and still had years of work ahead. He turned away. He was gone.

# *Epilogue*

O N HER TWENTY-FIRST BIRTHDAY, JESS CAME DOWN
to breakfast in the house she was sharing with three
other students, and found a pile of cards and a parcel
waiting for her. She was late as usual. She sat at their
rather dingy kitchen table, trying to eat a piece of toast,
drink a cup of coffee and examine the loot at the same
time. The others rushed around her, bundling into coats
and scarves and gloves. It was bitterly cold outside, and
not very warm in here – they couldn't afford much
heating. There was a card from Mum and Dad and Paddy
(young skinflint, you'd think he could have sent his
own), with a cheque. A card from Adam, who was no
longer under a death sentence: he'd started to work his
way through medical school. A card from Gran; one from
Noelle, with a letter. And a small parcel. It had a French
postmark. It had been addressed to her home in London.
Someone – Dad – had readdressed it and sent it on. Jess
stared at her own name, in old-fashioned copperplate
handwriting.

'Jean-Luc,' she murmured.

They had not kept in touch, not really. There didn't seem any point. He was Dr Batiste, the great scientist; he was old. They couldn't meet the way they had met in the garden . . . She remembered the elderly man at the back of the chapel, that day in Rochers: who had got up and hurried away when she looked round. It must have been that same day that Jean-Luc dropped his precious brocade bag through the grille over the *oubliette*-pit, to be found by Jess . . . It was odd to think that apart from that brief glimpse of a stranger, she'd only met him once: for one single hour in the waking world. They had been through so much together! Or so it had seemed, for that strange interlude. Jess had not forgotten. But she'd come to accept that she would never see or hear from her Jean-Luc again.

She opened the parcel, lifted a layer of wadding, and discovered an eighteenth century enamelled snuff-box. In a frame of leafy branches, two painted figures smiled at each other: the girl in gold-sprigged green skirts and a gold petticoat; the young gentleman in blue and rose; a dainty-looking sword at his side. She had seen them before. She had picked this box up and examined it, in Dr Batiste's house in Rochers, long ago. There was nothing else, no card, no message. She turned the snuff-box over and found a new inscription on the gold of the base:

*J. et J. Toujours.*

'That's pretty,' said one of her housemates, leaning over to take a look. 'Hey, what's up Jess? Seen a ghost?'

'No,' she said. 'Not a ghost . . .'

'Come on then, birthday girl. We are LATE!'

Jess jumped up, gobbling toast. She took her present, its wrapping and her cards, ran upstairs and shut them safely in her room. She ran down again, piled on outdoor clothes, grabbed her books and her bag and rushed into the snowy morning . . . into the everyday world; into her life.

But on the enamel snuff-box the girl in the gold-sprigged skirts was smiling still at the boy in rose and blue. Those lovers would be together in their garden, as they had been through the wars and revolutions. Whatever happened, that wouldn't change. There is a world where Time is not. Always.

## Author's Note

Though the type of illness, and the strategy described for gene therapy, have parallels in real life, there is no such disease as Sales' Myasthenia. Nothing stated about the imaginary disease, its causes or treatment, should be taken as scientific fact. The town of Rochers and the château of Rochers-Jumeaux are imaginary, but features of the fictional château and its traditions can be found at the Château Royale of Loches; the Châteax de Joux, Jura; and in the citadel of Besançon.

## Acknowledgments

For the historical background to Jean-Luc's story, I relied on Paul Webster's excellent book *Pétain's Crime* (Pan/Macmillan 1992). I'd like to thank Peter Gwilliam, for advice and support; Rita and Des Jones, who read the manuscript and provided helpful comments and corrections; and Gabriel Jimi Jones, to whom I told the story of Jean-Luc and the children, when we were travelling in France in the stormy summer of '93.